GW00692121

Twist and Shout

Twist and Shout

A Novel by
Philip Davison

BRANDON

First published in Ireland 1983
by Brandon Book Publishers Limited
Dingle, Co. Kerry.

British Library Cataloguing in Publication Data
Davison, Philip
  Twist and shout.
  I. Title
  823'.914[F]   PR6054.A896

  ISBN 0-86322-022-3

*The verse quoted on page 33 is from 'What About Us' by Jerry Leiber & Mike Stoller,
performed by The Coasters on the Atlantic record label, and is reproduced by permission of
Carlin Music Corporation.*

This book is published with the assistance of the Arts Council (An Chomhairle Ealaíon).

Typesetting: Leaders Phototypesetting, Swords, Ireland
Printed and bound by Biddles Ltd, Guildford, England

Chapters

for Nell

Chapter 1

PAR AVION

O<small>H, JESUS</small>, I said to myself, she's wearing the white gloves. Remember, you've only two choices now. You can't change course mid-way. Don't go to one of the others; it's too late. If you do, she'll call you over. You can either put it on the counter in front of her and act indifferent, or keep walking and let her call you over if she wants. Don't change your pace – not too fast, but don't linger. If you linger it will seem you are indecisive. The first option, I decided.

"Could you open it please, sir?"

I was going to, you silly cow.

"Yes." They never recognize the saxophone player. Smile if you can, I told myself, then open it. Give her more than she asks for. Open everything. Unzip the lot and stand well back.

She's not the sort of girl people write songs about, I said to myself. It's an expresso coffee pot, madam. Yes, it comes out there. Yes, and the lid works on a hinge. She's unscrewing it. She's looking down the little pipe. I don't believe this. Wait till she gets her hands on the Mickey Mouse watch. She'll pull his arms off. I wish I could have quoted a passage of Shakespeare at her.

Go near that polythene bag, madam, and you're fucked. I don't do my own laundry.

I determined that if she got snotty I would have a rummage myself and ask her had she not found it yet. She lost interest. She did not bother with my saxophone case.

The interior of the taxi I took from the airport across Dublin city was decorated with a dust-covered string of faded plastic flowers and religious frippery. The driver asked what nationality I was.

"I'm a problem child," I said coldly. I did not want to talk.

"I thought you were an Italian on account of the dark glasses and all," he replied and proceeded to tell me a ridiculous story about an encounter he had had with the Italian proprietor of a fish 'n' chipper.

" 'What's a chicken?' I says to the Italian. He looks at me with his mouth open. 'What's a chicken?' I ask again. The Italian jumped up and down doing his little chicken act and making chicken noises. 'What the Jaysus?' says I in amazement. All I wanted to know was how much a chicken cost." The taxi driver laughed loudly.

"I'm late," I said.

There was no escaping the fact that I was home. I glanced at the newspaper which the driver had made no attempt to fold when I disturbed him, but had stuffed between seats. At the bottom of the front page there was a report of a riot in London. 'BLACK AND WHITE YOUTHS RIOT IN BRIXTON' it read. Black and white youths?

For me, living in Ireland was like trying to breathe in through my nose and out through my mouth at the same time – it *should* be possible, but isn't.

If you are talented and you want success there comes a time when you panic. Did you ever accidentally turn on the cold tap with your toes after the water has run out of the bath? – it's that kind of panic. The remedy is immediately apparent. You do not want to leave under such circumstances, but you must.

"Get out of my way," you shout, looking back over your shoulder.

The taxi driver protected his investment by avoiding a pot hole. Taxi drivers all over the world do it, but in Ireland it is calculated that if the little holes are left alone long enough commuters will map them as hazards and consequently avoid them. Larger holes in the roads and pavements we do not fill in at all. We move them around or join them up to make bigger ones.

The church was almost full. I was content to take a seat in the third last row. To date, I have not sat in the top three-quarters at any wedding. Everyone was standing. Most were singing. There were a few spectators. Most were supporters. I had forgotten to pick up a programme at the door. I decided I had to have one. I disturbed the warbling woman next to me and walked back to the table, observed as I went by one of Avril's brothers who stood at the back of the church. I stared back at him. It's easy with dark glasses. He looked away.

Only when I had returned to my seat did I realize that I was holding a printer's blank. I smiled. Avril had arranged it, I was sure. She would be pleased to know that I got the joker. Without me detecting even a glance in my direction, the warbler took from her pretty daughter a programme and covertly offered it to me. I took off my glasses to say thank you. She did not respond so I put them back on and kissed the old bag on the cheek. She stood on her daughter's plastic sandals as she shrank away.

At the bottom left of page one it read: 'Avril'; at the bottom right: 'John'. I was very late. Already, they had reached the staples in the programme. Directly in front of me a child, resting on her father's shoulder, was examining his balding head. I could not clearly see what was happening at the altar. I could not see what they were doing to Avril.

I surveyed the congregation in search of familiar faces. I could identify a handful I had been to school with – now junior bank officials wearing badly fitted suits and broad ties – you can see them on their lunch break walking three abreast with their hands in their pockets. One is always making the other two laugh.

I was relieved to catch sight of Albert grinning at nothing in particular. You couldn't miss Albert. He is our West Indian. The last time I saw him was at the official opening of Bob's 'new studio'.

"Get that nigger out of here," says Bob, guffawing through cigarette smoke. "Look, he's eating a banana."

"Hold that," replies Albert, smiling. He hands Bob the banana and shows Bob and me a model of a sculpture he is working on.

"Is that what the world is coming to?" says Bob.

"Do you like it?" asks Albert.

"It's alright," says Bob, taking a piece of tobacco leaf off his tongue with his thumb.

"Big money," says Albert.

"Are you going to sign it 'Albert' across the base?" asks Bob.

"Oh yeah," replies Albert, looking at Bob's boots. He starts to laugh.

"Yeah, well at least I'm white," says Bob with a snorty laugh. "For three months before these all I had was a pair of Wellingtons."

Bob makes no distinction between practical and imprac- tical. He is a producer of outstanding examples of extremes of both. His creative imagination demands only effectiveness. In the house in Dun Laoghaire he had neatly papered every square inch of the walls of his toilet with blue and white 'Par Avion/ Aerphost' stickers – over twenty thousand of them. It took only a month to collect the quantity required. He visited most post offices on the south side of the city – some more than once – simply asked for a sheet of airmail stickers and was usually given several sheets at each. Bob modestly refers to it as 'strong wallpaper'. Albert swore that once he got lost in the little room because of its hypnotic effect. I would call it addictive. It was the first thing I checked had not been changed when later I went to visit Rene.

Chapter 2

NUMBER ONE

THE CEREMONY was almost over and I still had not seen the groom, frontal or profile. John what? *Missus* what?

"I bet he's got dandruff on his shoes," I said to myself.

When they came down the aisle under the spell her eyes were fixed on the rose window. It was the first time I saw her face since I arrived. She used to say that I had a weak smile. I wanted her to look in my direction to show her that I had not changed. Like the guilty man in an identity parade, I shook a little. I hated myself for doing so. She did not look my way. I kept my eyes on her as she passed. I couldn't help smiling my thin smile. The last time I touched her body was in my apartment in Berlin. I plugged the telephone answering machine into a wall socket and entered the bathroom. Avril was having a shower before leaving for Tegel Airport. I put the machine in the empty wash-hand basin, placed the microphone facing the shower, turned the volume to full and switched on to record. I reached behind the plastic curtain and danced my fingertips across her smooth, wet skin. She shrieked, then, laughing, she turned the water jets on me. I leaned back towards the microphone and recited my telephone number.

"We're all in the shower right now, but if you would like

to leave a brief message and your telephone number, I'll call you back."

Damn fool I was, making jokes when I should have said I loved her.

I met Bob outside the church.

"Number one," was his greeting.

"Yeah, number one down the pub," I replied. "How are you?"

"Ah," said Bob.

"Still haven't organized anything, have you?" I said. "It'll be alright when your ship comes in, right Bob?"

"The submarines are out. I think they got it. Backbone, that's what I need. Where can I borrow a backbone?" He nodded towards the church. "What do you make of it?"

"It doesn't matter much now, does it?" I replied. Bob was wearing his 'sporting gentleman's attire' jacket. "Where's the suit?" I asked, enquiring after his grey flannel suit which came out only for large gatherings and visits to the Arts Council.

"Adolf got it."

"Where's Adolf?"

"Dead. Died in action."

I had been looking forward to seeing Adolf again.

Chapter 3

ADOLF

HIS ˙FINEST hour was perhaps during the bizarre and dangerous recovery of a certain piece of sculpture which Bob had executed and sold to a wealthy pub owner in Letterkenny. It was a giant lobster made of numerous movable parts carved in wood and joined with rubber and bolts. In desperation, he had sold it at far too low a price and now it was vital that it be exhibited at the opening of the studio. His interpretation of the terms of sale was his justification for the robbery.

"He knew he had me at a disadvantage," Bob explained to me. "*He's* the robber."

To my surprise, the Mini took us – Bob, Adolf and myself – all the way to Donegal with only one stop to cater for mechanics. We had to piss in the radiator. It was not an easy feat. It required tenacity.

In contrast, the break-in, which took place while the pub was closed, was extraordinarily simple. It was only as we left with the great lobster that we were challenged by the owner who advanced with clenched fists and elbows drawn back. He shouted words neither of us could understand. Their aggressive tone, however, rendered understanding superfluous.

The moment Bob caught sight of him he dived into the car to avoid identification, dragging the lobster in after him. I had the thing by the tail. I pushed whilst looking over my shoulder. I had no qualms about kicking the brawny publican. I had seen enough dance-hall fights to know that they cannot be afforded. I took solace in the fact that he was 'culchie' – a farmer's son – who would not be prepared to fight as dirty or as fast as a city rocker. Even so, I was anxious about Bob effecting an escape that would include me.

In the event, I had only to hold the publican at bay with a boot. Adolf leapt from the car and savaged the publican's ankle. The combination of surprise and ferocity rendered the man frozen beef, but at the same time Bob took off down the road holding his door open and shouting Adolf's name, leaving me stranded. I ran after him. He did not stop until obscured from the publican's view by a hedgerow skirting a bend in the road.

"Adolf!" he shouted, not "Terry."

I clambered into the car and fought with the lobster for room. Presently, Adolf came running down the road and jumped into the car, panting contentedly. Because we could not see the publican we had no idea whether or not he was still alive. The price we paid for the engagement was the loss of a lobster leg for which I was blamed.

☆   ☆   ☆   ☆

"Great fellas, those," said Bob pointing to his opened programme as we left the church. I glanced at what he wanted to draw my attention to. It was Psalm 84.

"What fellas, Bob?" I asked.

"Great fellas. Couldn't do without them."

He was hardly alluding to Russian missiles, was he?

"Those fellas," he said, jabbing at a word. We stopped at the church gates. I looked. *Thine* was the word at the end of his finger. I took off my glasses and looked at Bob.

"Thine *who*, Bob?"

"No," he replied and again jabbed at the page, but with more precision. " 'I's," he said, pointing to the 'i' in *thine*. "Great fellas. Couldn't do without 'i's."

"Albert," I said, "did you save any of the stuff you two

have been smoking?"

"He's right," replied Albert, still grinning. "I and I know he's right."

I was glad that I had my glasses to put on because I could not think of anything to say.

"I have your old flat, Terry," said Albert. "I've made some awful improvements."

"Can't wait to see them, eh Terry?" said Bob.

"I'm not goin' near the place. I still owe a month's rent."

Bob's Mini has elasticated imitation leopard skin seat covers. The driver's seat was tilted forwards, resting on the steering wheel, dead or asleep. I sat in the back, Albert in the front. The engine started on the second attempt. I told Bob to drive to the Royal Hibernian Hotel. To counter my accusation that he had no intention of giving thought to organizing his life, he replied that he intended walking into the hotel one day with his full portfolio under his arm, trip, and when his work scattered on the floor, he would gather it quickly in a distressed state shouting, "No no, none of them are for sale!"

I had reserved a room by telephone from London. I'm not sure why. Perhaps it was to prove that this place – home – was remote; that this city could accommodate me only as a visitor. I wanted privacy and distraction. If I chose, I did not have to use the hotel room, just pay for it.

We were late. I left my clothes on the bed, took in the view from my window for a moment, shaved with my cut-throat, searched in vain for my toothbrush, hung the 'Do Not Disturb' on the door handle and returned to the car, which we had to push start. I pushed at the back. The boot, where my saxophone was, looked like the sort of place that smelled. It did smell. I had the full benefit. It smelt like dirty damp jeans had been stored there in a compress for a year. The door of the boot fell open when the engine caught. There was no way of securing the broken lock in the time available. I should have transferred my saxophone to the back seat and risked the case coming into contact with the sticky mess left on the seat by the piece of junk that had become part of a recent sculpting by Bob.

"It'll be alright," Bob said. "I'll be careful."

His words confirmed that I should not have come.

"You were asking about the studio, Terry," he said. "We've been having a spot of trouble with the postman. Albert, show him the letter," he said simpering.

Albert rummaged on the dashboard and gave me the letter. It was from the director of a small gallery, addressed to Bob.

> *Dear Mr. Clarke,*
>
> *I wish to express to you in the strongest possible terms our disgust at the behaviour of yourself and your guest at the opening of the Hopkins exhibition on Wednesday last. It is regrettable that your display of ill-manners leaves me no alternative but to inform you that we cannot allow you to exhibit in our gallery as had been planned for the month of October this year.*
>
> *Yours sincerely,*

Bob and Albert rejoiced in me saying emphatically: "No, I'm not going to ask."

"That's only the start of it," said Bob, but he did not elaborate.

The front passenger window rattled freely behind the door panel. Albert's flimsy jacket sleeve flapped like a flag in a gale as we drove along the Rock Road towards Dun Laoghaire.

Dublin Bay stays the same, just new versions of old political slogans are painted on the railway wall. A large portion of land overlooking the bay between Sandymount and Blackrock is owned by the church. I recall travelling on a bus full of blessers. Only Gaelic-speaking Catholic leprechauns are not under threat.

Dun Laoghaire is home territory – not the worst place to come from. I can say that now. 'The pouting rock 'n' roller' the local 'heads' used to call me – an attribute for a saxophone player.

"Very slick he looks now," they'll say, "playin' with the big boys. Always said he'd be a success. He deserves it, I suppose."

I do, but it's more fun when you think you don't deserve it.

"You don't put talcum powder in your hair anymore when you don't want to wash it, do you?" Rene will say when she sees the oil I've put in my hair.

Bob pulled into a petrol station where I had worked as a PPA (Petrol Pump Attendant). Being a PPA was part of it all and made me a better musician, some would say – not I. Bob refused to turn off the engine on the grounds that it would not start again. He offered a stern refusal and token abuse when the PPA laid down the orders he had been given.

"Upstart," I shouted, leaning forward to the open window. "You don't know your station in life." He wasn't sharp-tongued like I was when I held a petrol gun. I suppose I was hoping he would be. Instead, he was moronic. Eventually, Bob filled the tank himself while Albert kept his foot on the accelerator. I had to pay.

"I intend being controversial," said Albert as we pulled away.

"At the reception?" asked Bob.

"I intend being controversial," replied Albert. "Controversial people don't have money problems."

"Listen," said Bob, recognizing Albert's ascent into a creative mood – Albert can be difficult when he is creating – "at this thing we'll play for a draw."

Albert was quick to reply: "There is no need to use the hospital 'we' – *we*'ll play for a draw. I'm not going to make a scene. I like Avril. I'd drive without indicators for Avril."

"Oh God," said Bob.

☆　　☆　　☆　　☆

"Look," said Bob, pointing to the car in front, "that woman has a pixy in the passenger seat." I thought Bob might have grown out of this sort of drama, but he had not. He would never, nor would he cease to find fresh material. Bob spared no effort to overtake the vehicle. Having drawn level, it seemed to take two minutes to pass it. "It's against the law to steal garden gnomes!" Bob shouted through his open passenger window at the woman whose child was wearing an anorak with a pointed hood.

Bob does not have the menace in him that I have or Adolf had. I am a passionate hater.

Adolf used to piss on absolutely everything. He was an angry dog, a scrapper. He had characteristics that are lacking in Bob. Perhaps that is why it was an equable partnership. I have learned a lot about human nature from Adolf.

There was nothing Adolf hated more than the sight of himself. On seeing his reflection he would stop and remain still. He would watch intently, with his jaw slack. He would not breathe. The instant he detected a movement he would attack.

It is not difficult to visualize what happened when he caught sight of himself in the lens of the photo cabinet in Woolworth's where Bob and I had taken him to be photographed. It was my idea, I admit. I wanted the four poses of Adolf in my pocket for the duration of my exile.

He could not be contained. The warrior lunged from the stool on which Bob had pressed him into a seated position at the reflection. The first of the four flashes sent him scurrying out of the cabinet. In the aisle, he barked his fiercest at the machine with its insides flashing. The manager picked him up as though he were retrieving a runaway clockwork toy. Adolf squirmed. The manager was left holding the dog's tail. Just as small people dislike being touched, dogs with short tails are sensitive about tail abuse. Adolf had a starting handle for a tail – it looked like one and acted like one when grasped. Merely by holding the tail the good natured manager unwittingly had unleashed a gnashing ball of rage on his staff and customers.

We were at the hardware end of the shop. Because the man had Adolf under his arm before fear gripped him, he tossed certain injury away from his body rather than dropping it. The dog suffered a bad landing among a display of cheap vanity mirrors. Adolf was surrounded, but he was determined to give a good account of himself. Each bark lifted him, stiff-legged, off the ground. He catapulted himself at each mirror that caught his reflection. Without serious challenge from human beings, he thrashed his way from one end of the counter to the other, advancing and retreating, barking and biting. Each bark – each burst of hot, smelly breath – was directed at something. At the end of the counter he jumped to the floor and ran amuck at the front of the shop. He sprang onto the foot-plate of the large red weighing scales, effected a ninety-degree turn without reducing speed, leapt to the floor and hurtled along the plate glass doors. He clearly intended racing an entire lap of the shop perimeter. This was his undoing. An old lady entering the shop opened one of the doors. Adolf did not know what hit him. Such was the impact that the old lady was ejected into the street from where she came. Adolf sat down just before meeting the glass chest-on and bounced a clear three feet. Bob and I saw our chance to get out of the situation without being prosecuted. We approached rapidly. Adolf was docile. In fact, he was senseless. However, as Bob grabbed him by the scruff of the neck and pulled, he caught sight of his reflection in the stainless steel frame on the bottom of the door. *Now* he knew what had hit him. He made a token attack on the door as Bob pinned him under his arm and ran out of the shop with me close behind.

Chapter 4

HORSE THIEVES
AT THE RECEPTION

IT WAS early evening. The light revealed the ribs in car windscreens. Bob pointed to geese flying in V formation over the city heading out to sea.

"Good day tomorrow," he said.

"Watch the road," I replied. This almost caused an accident.

Albert was forced to stop fixing with a disfigured roll of yellow sellotape a torn pound note we had got in change at the petrol station.

"You should stick to tellin' tomorrow's temperature from today's tap water," said Albert to Bob. "That's what he does, you know."

"Who's car is this?" asked Bob indignantly.

"I hope my saxophone didn't fall out back there," I said.

When Bob pulled up at the deckchair-striped canvas-covered door, Albert was the only one taking in our surroundings.

"Do you think they know we're here?" he asked, straining to hear the crowd at the back of the large house.

I immediately checked that my sax was still in the boot. Bob checked, too. He pretended not to be anxious. This was difficult for he knew that he and the sax were of equal value to me. It *was* in the boot.

"You see," he said, yanking it out of the boot. The case opened and my sax fell out onto the gravel drive. The rough ride had released the loose catches on the case. Bob stood looking at it. I looked at Bob. Albert hopped out of the Mini and pretended to throw a tantrum in order to save Bob's life.

"Jesus, you Philistine," he said, pushing Bob around. "Wreckin' our best friend's livelihood. Jesus, you rude boy! You spoil everything just when it was all goin' so smooth. Fuckin' no musical appreciation at all," he said earnestly. Bob nodded 'yes' to everything.

A minor dent in the bell and a bent key was the damage. I cursed Bob, then myself for not having shouted at him when he reached for it; for not having had the catches on the case replaced; for not having been a paranoiac nursing the instrument in my lap.

The hall door was partially open. I wanted to be first to enter and I was. The brass knob had been warmed by the sun; a reminder to me to show no emotion.

Avril's parents were complacency on four legs. Her father was in a particularly jolly mood. Bob they were familiar with, but not me. Bob used to call to their house regularly, sometimes staying even when Avril was not there. Visiting the O'Connors was his knocking on the door of what he considered to be normality. He would wander about the household on display, bearing his smile that consistantly broke into a snorty, nervous laugh. He was completely taken by being such a source of entertainment, merely by turning up on the premises. He chose to interpret this as acceptance; reassurance that if he ever needed to change he would have models. He still cannot see that his acceptance depends on him being in the state of disarray he will forever exist in. In Avril's eyes am I any different? Am I not just less funny, more ruthless?

I had met Mr O'Connor several times before, each occasion for the first time as far as he was concerned. His business required that he travel regularly. The last occasion I met him was at the opening of Bob's studio. Avril was standing with Bob. She was complimenting him on the shine on his ageing pair of 'sensible' shoes. He, apparently, was preoccupied with the notion that for one reason or another, his eyesight was adrift.

"I'm sure one of them is darker than the other," he said in a serious tone.

"Robert, I wouldn't know you in your new suit!" said Mrs O'Connor pleasantly, as she and her husband joined our group in the overgrown yard outside the studio (Bob is never to be found playing host at his own receptions and parties).

"Oh, it's not new, Mrs O. The person who owned it isn't with us any more. Have you looked at the prints yet? Very good value," Bob said hunching his shoulders as he drank wine from his glass.

"Oh yes, very good," said Mr O'Connor with a nod that referred to the prints on the studio walls.

Bob was enjoying all the attention. He introduced me – yet again – to Mr O'Connor then told him: "Go in there and shell out."

Now, at the wedding reception, Mr O'Connor lifted my hand from my side and shook it vigorously. He could not remember my name. He congratulated me, having had some vague recollection of his daughter ordering him to do so for reasons he had momentarily forgotten.

"Pop star, isn't that right!" he blustered, eyeing me from head to foot. "Look at the pink socks!"

"What about your beer belly, mister?" I said. "I can take my socks off." I gave him my best alligator smile.

"Well, I call a spade a spade, Barry ... " said Mr O'Connor to me.

"Terry, dear," said Mrs O'Connor, correcting her husband. "His name is Terry."

"Terry!" said he to his wife, then turned again to me. "I call a spade a spade, and quite honestly, Terry, I'm glad my daughter didn't marry you." The mildness in his voice thinly disguised the fact that he was angry. "You people have success too early in life. You're not ready for it."

"What do you say to that, Terry?" asked Mrs O'Connor. "He's saying that our son-in-law is the better man." She enjoyed teasing.

"People who call a spade a spade don't say they call a spade a spade," I said addressing her, pushing my glasses up the bridge of my nose with one finger. "What's for dinner, Mrs O'Connor? Roasted underdog?"

☆   ☆   ☆   ☆

Avril's mother, who sleeps with rolled up newspaper in her beehive hair-do, introduced me to the groom's parents as a pop star friend of her daughter.

"Doesn't he look like an international swimmer?" she commented pleasantly.

The groom's mother politely asked if I had seen the swimming on the television.

What *is* this about? I asked myself. I can't even fuckin' swim.

"Swimming, as a sport, is for morons, madam," I said. "It's like marvelling at how well chickens fly."

There was a beat before she laughed.

"We have a band, you know," said Avril's mother nervously to *me*.

I looked around as I said: "Oh yeah?" I could not help recalling seeing a workman singing 'My Delilah' down a large pipe suspended from a digger. I wondered had I imagined the telephone call from Mac saying that he and the boys were playing at the wedding and asking if I were coming would I blow sax.

☆   ☆   ☆   ☆

"Hello, who are you?" I snapped at the small boy who stood with his fingers in his mouth, staring up at me.

"I'm George Nugent's child."

Bob choked on a cough. Albert grinned.

"Oh God help you," I said as compassionately as I could.

George Nugent and his wife, Clare, approached. Bob

recognized them first.

"How are you?" Bob asked. "See the nipper's still alive," he said nodding to the small boy.

"I don't think they get the joke," Albert said to me in a low voice. He was right.

In the early days of their marriage Bob and I took advantage of George and Clare regularly. Newly married couples known to you are always good for a free dinner. Offer to do house painting or the like and you'll get an invitation. Dinner out of new pots onto new plates and into your stomach.

☆   ☆   ☆   ☆

"Oh Jaysus," said Bob, "not the short story writer."

"Poet," said Albert correcting him. "He's a copy-writer with an advertising agency. Go a-way you copy-writer, you," said Albert before the approaching entity was within earshot. I heard and felt him before I saw him.

"*Hey*, Terry Hatchel!" he said slapping his hand on my shoulder. "Good lad!"

"*Good lad?*" I muttered, turning to stare.

"I hear you're living in London. What part?" He was all open and friendly.

"Near the middle," I said curtly.

"Listen . . . great stuff, I understand. What are you doing at the moment?"

"We're at a wedding reception, right?" I asked Albert. Albert nodded 'yes'. "I'm at a wedding reception," I said addressing the intruder. He must have got the message, but he merely changed the subject.

"Have you known Avril and John long?" he asked with a wide smile.

"You ask a lot of questions, don't you?" I said. "I don't know who you are."

"Oh, I didn't mean to hassle you," he said all concerned, and introduced himself.

"Alright," I replied and turned away.

'It's just I've been doing a bit of song-writing myself," he said following me. "I must talk with you sometime."

"No, not with me," I told him.

"You heard him," said Albert indicating with a twitch of his head that he should piss off.

"Did you see his rotten teeth?" Bob asked after he had moved away. "He must have born in the forties when there was less calcium in the water."

☆　　☆　　☆　　☆

There were three of them, sixteen or seventeen years old, each of them attractive like the girls who sing hymns on television – the innocent ones you want to touch; the ones who know you want to touch them; the ones who want to touch. One stuck out her breasts as she pulled her jumper down around her waist. The one with the bright eyes would have put her tongue in my ear if I had glanced sideways. They loved *everything* about me, they and their attractive bodies said. There wasn't *anything* they didn't want to know. They'd go anywhere with me. I told them I was a musician, that I hated flying in jets, hated swimming pools, didn't lie in the sun and frequently suffered from exhaustion and insomnia.

"I'm forced to be a nomad, a user of fifty different brands of soap," I explained. God, how modest I was!

Did I swim in other famous people's swimming pools, then? I told them I could not swim and, of course, instantly I had three offers to teach me how.

"You've got the wrong one," I said. "Your Da earns more than I do. The fella who sings is the big star." I was banking on them asking me about him. I was prepared to enjoy telling them a harmless pack of lies that I knew would delight them.

"Oh no!" they insisted, I was not the wrong fella. I'd do fine! Then we were interrupted. Gillian arrived.

She positioned herself in front of me before sitting down at the table. She introduced her gentleman friend then ignored him thereafter, just as she ignored those I was talking with. She told me she was pleased to be sitting beside me. She's one of those who, at dinner and cocktail parties, tells you, a stranger, all about herself and her snobby preferences and doesn't notice she is spilling her drink down your trouser leg. Eventually, she will be an old lady with a small, smelly dog.

"Glad I'm here, are you, Gillian?"

She rose to the challenge. She was such an easy target.

"Naturally," she said, sitting down on my right. She expected me to move the saxophone case off the chair for her. I made her do it herself. She blew smoke in my eyes like they do in the prison camp pictures.

"Bob, isn't that where you're sitting?" I asked.

Bob was sitting on Albert's left and Albert was next to me on my left. He drew his chin into his chest and held his breath as he half stood to look across the table at the chair.

"Oh yeah," he replied with great exhaltation. "This one," he said pointing to the chair he had risen from, "is Albert's." He stood up straight and moved confidently round the table to Gillian where he waited. Albert moved onto the chair he had just vacated.

"And this one," I said pointing to the chair Albert had vacated, "is for Avril. She's coming over to talk to me."

"Oh, I see," she said unpleasantly. To abandon her escort now and move to where Albert had been sitting would have been trying too hard.

"I like her," said Albert after she and her docile friend had left the table as a result of my rudeness. "She's old for her age, you know what I mean?"

"Don't mistake squareness for maturity, Albert."

"I'd like to paint her, anyway."

☆   ☆   ☆   ☆

Somewhere about what I suspect was only half way through the best man's speech (he was clever and funny; his speech was not) a familiar cry went up. At first it was in a low voice, then it got louder. Concern became alarm.

"Where's moh horse?" The western twang in the voice was exhilarating. I responded.

"Hey, where's *moh* horse?" I said, then, with alarm: "Has anyone seen moh horse?"

Necks stretched. Heads turned. Mouths made shapes

and mumbled. The best man faltered. Avril had to turn away to laugh. For her, too, it was a familiar call. Her husband was disgruntled.

"Where's moh horse?" Bob again demanded. Anyone who had been to see some of the lesser pictures in the Forum cinema when we were there smiled. This call was a sure sign that the tense moment had arrived.

It hadn't been planned for the wedding reception, but it is the kind of thing reunions produce. I was surprised and pleased at how rapidly we earned disgust. Equally, I was surprised at Bob's taking the interruption as far as an attempted coup.

"On behalf of the scruffier element here," he shouted archly, rising to his feet, "I would like to take this opportunity to express our heartiest congratulations to our dear friend, Avril." He was drunk, more drunk than I had realized. "However, we're not so sure about the other fella." The crowd's mumble became discontented muttering. The initial smattering of laughter had evaporated. "*But* . . . in fact, we, those of us who have just vocaled our presence, have lost more than our horses, we fear." Had Adolf bitten him before departing, I wondered. "There's no need for this." Suddenly, the person all had come to regard as a humorous distraction, a 'harmless character', was in earnest. Avril had stopped laughing. "There was no need for this, Avril."

Bob had stolen my private scene and performed it. I sat there with my mouth open, watching as two men seated near him tried to subdue him. They made him angry. Christ, I didn't even know he liked Avril. I saw Albert move towards him. Bob was getting physical. I got up and caught Albert by the elbow.

"What is he doing?"

Albert wasn't sure how concerned he should be. "He's not playin' for a draw, that's what."

Albert and I arrested Bob and took him into the house. The best man restarted his speech by appreciating Bob's joke.

☆   ☆   ☆   ☆

I decided I would make short my visit to Dublin. I asked Bob where the telephone was. I intended ringing my sister.

He advised me that the phone in the drawing room would be disconnected, as was customary when parties were held, and suggested that I use the extension in the master bedroom – Mrs O'Connor's bedroom – the phone, he claims, she took off the hook when she brought him there and got passionate the afternoon he called looking for Avril.

"Special privileges I have in this house, she said to me," said Bob, trying to nod away my doubt. "Very big on the arts, she is."

I found myself standing in the drawing room wondering did he really give it to her. No, not Bob. He would have run. The scene I imagined prompted me to lift the receiver in the drawing room. I noticed it smelt of perfume. It was a scent that reminded me of someone, I could not think of whom. Then I realized there was a dialling tone. I looked down at the small black connection box on the skirting board. The casing was off but the wires connected. It was Rosie's perfume I decided. I knew she regularly made calls from others' houses. I was sure she had reconnected the wires. I turned and surveyed the crowd. Mac had not told me she would be singing. I have a lot of time for Rosie, and she for other people. She's a cabaret singer. She dresses and makes up like a tart. She is the only woman I know who does it magnificently, and she looks great on the telephone.

☆   ☆   ☆   ☆

Rosie had followed us and stood in the kitchen doorway smiling at me. Some smiles you can ignore, although none you can forget. Rosie's you cannot ignore. It was the kind of welcome that creeps up under your clothes. She came to me, took off my dark glasses and kissed me. I wiped the lipstick from my lips, looked at it on my fingers.

"Rosie."

"Fish fingers are the only fish that don't give me the pip," declared Bob. "Fish are always lookin' at you with one eye, sometimes both."

He had put the goldfish in its bowl in the deep freeze. In half an hour, he explained, it would be suspended in a block of ice. Then he would put it back in its place in the corner of the kitchen where Mrs O'Connor kept it. He could position it so that the fish would be facing into the corner and would be unable to turn around and stare at him. When it thawed, he concluded, the fish would be dead and consequently would float to the surface where its stare would be concentrated on the bottom of the bowl and up into the air (having an eye on either side of its head), not at him.

Bob had cleared a space on the serving counter and made himself a mixed pickle sandwich-like object which he was now eating. He said he wouldn't be staying to hear me play. He claimed he had an important issue to raise with his fellow artists. Albert would drive him back to the studio and when the wedding reception got out of hand I was to go there too, taking with me whatever I could manage. He said his career was at stake, that I would understand. Albert looked at the ceiling and sighed.

The tangents Bob embarks on are incredible and very often funny. They are never calculated; usually untimely as a result. They are poignant, but obscure. They are always disconcerting. They have earned him the reputation for being insincere – wholly a fallacy.

"I wouldn't do that too often, Rose," said Bob, "you don't know where *his* mouth has been. He used to play desks in school – you know those cheap metal tube ones; he used to take the caps off the ends, bung a trumpet mouthpiece in and blow."

"I bet he got a couple of notes out of them," said Rosie looking me over approvingly.

Apparently, like Adolf in a restaurant, Bob was neither embarrassed nor inhibited by Rosie's show of affection for me. I knew better.

"Rose, you saw me in my underwear this morning," he said.

"Yeah."

"How was it for you?"

"Oh, pretty bad," Rosie said kindly.

☆　　☆　　☆　　☆

I saw Albert and Bob off the premises.

"This party is not for us any more," Albert had said finishing Bob's pickle sandwich for him. "I think we should go. Where's the telephone?" he asked.

"The one in the drawing room works," I said.

"I don't care whether it works or not. I'll be back in a minute, then Bob and I will go." He left the kitchen. He returned with Part Two of the telephone directory rolled tightly under his arm. "What you all lookin' at?" he said to Rosie and me. (Bob did not seem surprised and paid little attention.) "It's the country section. Nobody uses that. I could have lifted both."

Bob insisted on walking to the Mini with his 'sporting gentleman's attire' jacket over his head as though he were a controversial defendant being led out of a courthouse. Everyone looked. No one laughed, but even as Albert drove away, Bob, sitting in the back seat, maintained his cover.

I looked up at the sky when I saw Mrs O'Connor approaching. I wanted nothing to do with her.

"Poor Robert," she said as though he were being taken to a place I knew him to be escaping from. "Do you think it will rain on your lovely shiny hair?" she asked, concerned.

"Tarzan used hair-oil and water from the sky never messed up his, so if it rains, Mrs O'Connor, I'll be alright." She was actually captivated by my sarcasm. "The last time I was at an open-air wedding reception was with Bob and Avril and another girl. We had to drive a long way. We arrived late. We had to change our clothes on a golf course before going to the church. I think that was when Bob fell for your daughter, Mrs O'Connor."

Mrs O'Connor went away to think.

"Did that fella call round to you last night with no clothes on?" I asked Rosie, being quick to draw conclusions. Bob and his clothes were preying on my mind.

"No, I spent the night at Rene's. Someone has to be in a sober state to drive her to hospital."

"What?"

"Didn't Bob tell you – he should have – Rene is having a baby . . . his baby. Very soon."

"I was wondering where she was," I said, a lame response that did not disguise my surprise.

"Nobody told you?" asked Rosie. There was a pause. I did not reply. "And I always thought it was Avril," she said knowingly. Rosie always says the right thing. She had me smiling.

Rene was still living in a flat in the house where Bob and I had lived when he was in his final year at art school. He was still living in the house, too, but often slept in the studio. Albert, a frequent guest, was then and is now at art school. I had spent a year and a half there and left. Rene was the exception. She worked in the museum as a research assistant. The geography of her flat remains more vivid in my mind than that of my own. Because her window looked out onto the long, narrow back garden, she was appointed watcher of the plants. Half of Dun Laoghaire is under cultivation. It was no different then. We were very proud of our plants (and, given our financial position, quite dependent on them) and so kept a keen eye on them lest someone attempt a transplant. I admit, this was how we acquired our five plants in the first place. One bright afternoon we robbed the plants from a friend's window box. I did the robbery – he was Bob's friend. Bob drove. We had no plans as such, but instead had defined our attitude to the execution of the deed – before and during we would be confident, afterwards we would be smug. In the event, we anticipated the smugness driving through Dun Laoghaire with the five potted plants dancing in the windows of Bob's Mini.

It was one night while Rene glanced at the dark patch where she knew our plants to be, that she saw Jimmy at work for the first time. Jimmy still lives next door with his widowed mother. He's forty-five years old and holds his mother's hand when she goes shopping or visits the bookie. Jimmy is devoted to his mother, but by night he is preoccupied with something different. He robs clothes lines of female underclothing.

Local people consider it a serious threat. His territory is extensive. No one knows when and where he will strike.

We decided to photograph him in the act. We set a trap in our own back garden using some of Rene's lingerie. Afterwards, we decided to sell the photograph to the newspapers when we discovered that the bastard had trampled three of our five plants in his getaway. The newspapers, however, did not print the photograph. We had Jimmy enlarged and he has been hanging on the wall of Bob's studio ever since. Jimmy still goes out on the odd expedition, I understand, but his mother hasn't been well lately. I have the negative of the photograph. I'm saving it for an LP cover.

So, I would not be sleeping with Rene. Most of the time I took her for granted and now, I was trying hard not to do it again. The coffee percolator was for her. She always made lousy coffee.

☆ ☆ ☆ ☆

"I'm glad to have the opportunity to play, Rosie," I said. "It's my big chance to say: 'What about me?'," I said trying to be the fool.

She whispered – half sung – close to my ear a verse of a Coasters number:

> He's got a car made of suede
> With a black leather top
> If we go out on dates
> We go in a box on roller skates
> What about us?

"I'm richer than the lot of you," I said with counterfeit pride.

"Ah-ha!" said Rosie. "Money, money, money!"

"It's really coming together for me now, Rosie. I'm living the way I've always wanted to, playing better than I ever did . . . it's happened just a bit late, that's all."

"It can never happen fast enough, can it?" she said, trying to be kind.'

"I'm being silly over the woman, aren't I?" I said after a pause.

"Yes," said Rosie softly.

"I mean, Avril was never interested."

"Well, not anymore." There was another pause. "You think she didn't believe in you, Terry? That's why she didn't stay with you?"

"Something like that."

"So, you want to play for her now. You're not going to let her off lightly."

"Well, I had planned to play at the wedding service in the church ... just when he asks has anybody any objections I thought I'd cause a bit of anarchy."

"Mm, you should have," said Rosie. "*You'd* have got away with it."

"Do you think she would have minded?" I asked Rosie, pleased and encouraged by what she had said.

"No, but the others would have."

"To hell with them."

"You see, you *would* have got away with it!"

☆   ☆   ☆   ☆

In Avril's tea rooms there hangs a 1940s glossy advertisement. CRAVAN A – FOR THAT "EXTRA TOUCH OF QUALITY" it reads. The scene depicted is soft lit. The couple are in evening dress. There are roses on the table. The man leans forward with the table candle to light her cigarette. She is looking into his eyes and smiling. She is content to be with him. She is attentive. Not even the enormous, opened twenty pack floating in the corner can distract her. She is falling in love with him. All women I compare to her. If she sang, she'd sing like Rosie.

"What's the matter," asked Avril with a good humoured smile, "has some girl broken your heart?"

"I don't know," I replied. "I haven't looked yet." I detected a softness that has always been present in Avril's manner, but on this occasion I felt the effect of its continuity. It prompted me to introduce Joan to her.

Joan came with me to the tea rooms for the first time shortly before she left for Berlin where she was to join her boyfriend. I seem to be forever slipping down cracks that swallow those who turn up too late. It was pouring rain. I insisted on standing outside the shop looking in the window. I refused to explain to Joan that I was waiting to attract Avril's attention. I stood with my hands in my coat pockets, wearing the dark glasses I had just bought. I must have looked like a shop dummy left out in the rain. Joan tried to be patient.

"Are you trying to remember something?" she asked. "Are you looking for somebody? Why don't you knock on the window?"

Such was my concentration, I could have dismantled a thorn bush with my bare hands and not sustained a single scratch. Eventually, Avril looked in my direction. I kept my eyes on her and ignored Joan's distress. I pointed to Joan, mimed the snapping of an imaginary object, pointed to myself, then to my heart. I could see Avril frown, then laugh. The rain got heavier. Joan demanded an explanation. She was suddenly very annoyed. I take pleasure in lying to persons who are angry or annoyed. However, I was not deceitful in replying to Joan. I liked her too much for that. I told her I had indicated that I was broke and that she, Joan, would be paying.

"That's what you think!" she said.

"You bet!" I said.

"Avril is a good friend to you," Joan said when we had left the tea rooms. "When you were over talking to those people in the corner she sat down and talked with me . . . she was checking me out."

I couldn't help smiling.

"Yeah, she's my friend."

Chapter 5

BERLIN

I WENT to Germany with Mac and the Banisters. At the last moment one of the band couldn't travel because it would have cost him his job. I got to play bass, my second instrument, and occasionally, sax. I remember being very impressed with Mac. He had got them a booking in the Logo Club in Hamburg.

In all, we spent eight weeks in that city, barely surviving on what we earned from playing our best. (I was the only one who had any money saved when we left Dublin – this money I took with me for I was determined I would stay away as long as I could.)

Mac and the Banisters left no lasting impression and club owners who were willing to take a chance on us drawing became fewer and fewer. Mac found one who was willing to get us a gig or two in Berlin. We didn't ask how much we would be paid, just where the places were.

In my business you notice people being drawn together; how they work together, live together or fail to do either. You tend not to question what are sometimes unlikely and opportune circumstances.

I was so happy to see Joan again. She had been living in Berlin with her boyfriend for almost a year. He was one of three Englishmen living in that apartment building in the district of

Wedding. He came from Liverpool; said without malice that he knew all about the Irish. His wife was still in Liverpool, or perhaps in London. She would have tried to have taken their three-year-old daughter from him if she had known where they were. Joan had met him in London through Pete.

He worked as a roughneck on an oil rig: two week shifts-two weeks on the iron platform, two weeks with Joan and his daughter in Berlin; from the sea port that serviced the rig almost a day on the train across northern Europe into the Eastern Zone to Berlin; from one island to another.

Joan, with her part-time secretarial job at the American Institute, was content to wait for him. The effort she put into renovating their apartment attested to that contentment. He built for them a large loft bed underneath which was the toddler's cave where she slept.

It was easy for me to think Joan was the only person in Berlin. I knew that if I planned to stay any length of time in the city I would have to guard against believing such or worse, believing that I was the only person she knew.

I *did* stay a considerable time. Mac and the others shared a cramped and shabby apartment in Kreuzberg. Already, I was thinking about session work on my own, or being what is known in Berlin as a 'stripper' – a musician who plays in the clubs and rarely, if ever, in the studios. I did not share my money with the others in the band and had no conscience about it. With Joan's help I got an apartment for thirty pounds a month. Even without work I had enough money saved to last four or five months if I was careful.

There seemed to be a lot of floor space in my apartment. Was it because I furnished the living room with cheap garden furniture? I think it was because I was living alone. How well you know your rooms when you live alone.

There was one piece of furniture that had been left behind by the previous occupant – a broken telephone answering machine which I got repaired.

Like many flats in apartment buildings on the continent built before the Second World War, the windows of mine overlooked a courtyard. I was fortunate in having a small balcony with space for two chairs and racks to grow plants. The courtyard, from the fifth floor, was a well; a theatre of sorts that stretched sound. If ever a chamber were designed to treat notes from a saxophone, this was it ... if you dare play.

In one corner of the living room stood the tall, pillar-box-like stove with green tiles which I kept polished. Polishing the tiles preserved its radiant nature, although not once in the time I lived there did I light the stove. On the flat top I put a potted plant that was trying to be a work of art. Each sunny morning, for approximately an hour, there would be a patch of mottled silvery light on the wall adjacent, a projection of the hand-struck panes of glass in the window frames.

I had sent Avril a postcard:

Dear Avril

    Everything great. Can it last?
Better come here quickly.

                      Love,

                        Terry

It doesn't matter to me what the conditions are in the places I play. I care about the rooms in which I live; where I practice and wait to play. I wanted Avril to displace the placid atmosphere that had stood still since the bombs ceased to shake the building, as much as I wanted the place to contain her; to make her stay.

☆   ☆   ☆   ☆

The bookings the club manager in Hamburg had set up turned out to be five Sunday mornings playing in a pub. I got the worst spot on the cramped stage. It is the saxophonist's lot to get stuck out on one wing. If the stage has been temporarily extended with upturned beer crates or orange boxes he will be standing on them. I played my best in a hall in Carlow standing on a billiard table covered with boards.

Our five Sunday mornings paid enough for dinner and we had to put the tables and chairs out ourselves. We would arrive in the morning and find the chairs carelessly stacked upside-down on the tables – it was a lion-tamer's paradise.

Mac organised a demo recording to get us studio work. We went to an old building on Paul-Linke Ufer by the canal, and were slowly led through the neglected courtyard, then down into a dirty, damp cellar without windows. It cost us money and there was nothing of quality to listen to at the end of the session.

Mac got us another demo recording, this time in a proper studio. He had worked up an enthusiasm in an assistant engineer he had met at the Quasimodo. It was arranged that we would record on a Sunday morning. It was at that recording I was introduced to Otto Rollig, a producer. He happened to be in the studio building, heard my sax solo and like it. Otto Rollig couldn't read music. He employed an arranger to do his work, but I was grateful for his attention.

Musicians, club owners, promoters and technicians – everyone in the business in Berlin knows Ulli Toller, a short man with tinted glasses. He offered me his services as agent. I agreed. Most horn players in Berlin play in more than one band. It made sense that I do the same. If you are a musician looking for work with bands there you are sure to find listeners if you are from the US or England, and if you're from Ireland you're from England.

The few gigs Mac and the Banisters got were the most satisfying. We pretended we were on stage at the Magnet in Dublin and played what we wanted. We told the audiences to fuck off if they didn't like it.

Toller got me a lot of stripper work, most of it playing 'schlager' (musak) with German bands. It was tough work: 140 DM a night for four forty-minute sessions.

Often, on my way home in the small hours, exhausted and hungry, I would look in a particular cafe's windows and see flowers in slender vases on the tables, blooms that had been folded when I went to work and were now open, ready for the morning.

This work was the doldrums for me. Consistently, my longing to see the opened blooms came earlier each night. But even on the worst night every note matters. On the best night, the living in between each note is lost to the next.

It was easy to say nothing else mattered but the music. There were times when all I could do was blow. There were nights when I feared that no sound came out of the instrument. I had such a night before Avril arrived in Berlin.

Chapter 6

ONLY PLAYING

At TEGEL Airport the movement and sounds seemed endowed with extra clarity for my benefit alone. I enjoyed the waiting. I wanted her to be last off the plane. I watched from a distance her coming through the arrivals door. I watched her looking for me. She waved. She even called my name. I advanced slowly. I let her come to me. I had her full attention. I wanted to make it last.

Immediately, I noticed that Avril was wearing glasses. Later, I asked her about them. She told me she wore them only when her contact lenses hurt her such as in dusty conditions or, as was the case, if she had lost a lens.

"Do you not recognize me?" she asked warmly. "Do you not like them?"

"They make you look like one of those women in Alfred Hitchcock pictures who are irresistible when they take off their glasses and let down their hair. Of course, when you know they are that sort of woman they become irresistible with their hair up and glasses on."

"What *are* you talking about?" Avril asked bemused.

"Let me see," I said. "Let me try them on." Avril offered a doubtful frown. "Come on, come on," I said advancing and reaching for the glasses. I was determined to try them on. She closed her eyes when I took them off. "Do *you* like them?" I asked, putting them on and squinting in the mirror.

"Oh, I don't mind them."

They were strong. I did not realize before that the lenses she wore were so strong. She was near sighted. Perhaps that was why I was attracted to her eyes; they seemed so penetrating; they seemed to search at great depths.

"How can you see what they look like on you?" I asked.

"They are adjusted to suit *my* eyes, stupid!"

"Ahh, right," I said vacantly as I removed the glasses and, keeping my gaze fixed on the image in the mirror, squinted and opened wide my eyes to check I had done no damage to my vision.

Subsequently, in Berlin, she did not wear her glasses.

When Avril looked inside my fridge she was surprised, perhaps shocked, at the modest variety of baby food I kept there. It was for lean times, I explained to her, when I was out of work and had little money.

"Baby food is highly nutritious," I told her. "You can stretch it. It may not be appetizing, but it's better for you than corn flakes. You stay hungry, but healthy."

I was disappointed when she did not compliment me on what I knew to be resourcefulness. She was not surprised by the remaining contents of the fridge. She gave me her talk on malnutrition in bed-sit land while I stared into the fridge as though it had no back to it. She said that my kind of existence depressed her, often disgusted her. She said it was considerate of me to think of stocking up on sauce bottles and tubes, beer and sour milk for her stay. It's funny how men can warm to women who give such speeches. It's funny how women so often misconstrue your intentions. The door of my fridge was always exceptionally well stocked. The rest, I admit, was sparsely occupied. Truthfully, I deliberately left it spacious so that I could fill it with the kind of things she liked to eat. At the time, I wasn't sure what that might be. It never occured to me that this would be interpreted as negligence. It put me in mind of that annoying parable I had served to me in school with reverence –

about the three men who were given money by their boss: the first got three pounds, the second, two, and the third, one. When the boss came back from foreign parts number one and two had gone into business and had made a profit and were smug and got a pat on the back. The third saved his one pound and got fired for being a waster. The poor bastard thought he was a big success saving his quid. Like the PPA, he was moronic. He didn't know any better.

Chapter 7

SIXTY MAJOR

"HEY LISTEN, I'm ringing from a gobbler. I'm in the train station. Come and get me, quick." Bob had arrived.

From Dublin to Berlin overland was for him a long time to be among strangers in trains and boats and not to speak or laugh or sleep; to be his own company and not to work. In London he telephoned Pete. Everybody in Dublin knows someone who has moved to London. Pete has been there the longest of any of our friends. I grew up with him. I spent a lot of time at his house. We used to write pop songs in his kitchen after school. He is now a graphic designer. If you said 'Hatcher' (that's me) sent you, you'd be sure of a place to stay. Had Pete been at home in his flat Bob would probably have gone no further. He had second thoughts and almost turned back. I was proud of him for not having done so, cursing him for having come to Berlin at this time. He knew it when I met him with his nervous laugh that was also a smile. Together, Bob and I are two halves of the one person – the same half.

He stood on the street corner outside the Zoo Station casting a long shadow in the early morning light. Beside him was an American couple he had adopted, tourists with their bodies on back to front. The three looked like disorientated extras in a film who wandered off the set that is East Berlin on the far side of the wall.

"What the hell's a gobbler?" I snapped at him as I came up out of the pavement from the U-bahn.

"A telephone ... with one of those chutes that eats your money," he replied pointing back at the station.

"You're a right friend, you are, arriving like this ..."

More snorty laughter in response. "I nearly didn't find the place."

"I don't want to know how you got here."

"That train's going on to Moscow, ya know," he said ruefully.

I stretched my lips thin.

"I brought ya sixty Major," he said.

☆   ☆   ☆   ☆

Cigarettes are not all the crazy fool brought me.

"This is for your wall," he said in my apartment, giving me a print he had made. "I have a story for you: I was on the tear in town – making an eejit of myself in the dirty place and I got thrown out. Round the corner to the other one ..." He mimed a majestic arch from his fly to the floor. I rolled my eyes to the ceiling. He had been so drunk in the pub, he had pissed on the counter or in someone's empty glass. " ... 'Come on, out! OUT!' Out I went. I know this skiffer in a bedsitter in Rathmines, so I went down there to see her. There's a lot of bedsitters down there, you know. The door was open so I went in. It was very dark – couldn't see a thing. She wasn't in so I went asleep. When I woke up there was a policeman's uniform hanging on the end of the bed and two pairs of motorbike gauntlets on the floor. So I stole the policeman's gauntlets and brought them to the studio and did a print of them." That was the print he was now giving to me. "I call it 'James Joyce's Motorbike Gauntlets'."

Avril, Bob and my birthday had arrived together. It was almost too much to cope with.

Chapter 8

MY BIRTHDAY

I THOUGHT I'd use the 'scream in the library' tactic.

"It's *my fucking birthday* today," I said. "It's *my* day. Terry Hatchel Day. I want attention."

On the way back from the park I bought the brat a red lollypop the size of a badmington racquet. We stopped to buy groceries in a sheltered market. The shopping list was divided and we separated: Joan, the toddler and the pram, Avril and myself.

Neither Avril nor myself can speak much German. We did a lot of pointing. We had trouble with the kilos. Worst of all, however, was buying the minced meat. Minced meat is not always on display in German butcher shops. They mince while you wait. It is very hard to mime minced meat.

Until it came to the minced meat Avril was successfully doing all the buying. She tried explaining in English and French at the first butcher's stall, but to no avail. At the second, I made a serious effort. She was no help at all. She stood comically transfixed by a mean un-Aryan looking rocker with a smear of motorbike grease on his bare, enormous Buddha belly which blocked one half of the passageway. I admit, I looked at the figure more than once. Not even at the Magnet in

Dublin had I seen such an ugly rocker. These people are fortunate in having so little explaining to do, I thought. Bob would have wanted to paint him had he seen him. He would have made a great LP cover.

Eventually, we successfully purchased, among other things, minced meat, and reunited with Joan. She put some of the groceries in the net basket attached to the pram. Avril and I split the remainder between us. It was really quite a load. Without doubt, it was the end of an era for my fridge. Much of what we had bought would only be partly used in the dinner that was planned at my place. Joan's neighbours, the two other Englishmen living in her apartment building, were invited. They being homosexuals, Joan was convinced they would be very fussy about dinner, hence the elaborate preparations (whatever about the queers, with such vast expenditure I intended acting very fussy).

"Nobody remembered my birthday and when I remind you you invite strangers to my hastily arranged party," I said dolefully. "And Bob, he spends the day sleeping."

Joan and Avril laughed conspiratorially. Avril took hold of my arm with her free hand. She kissed me on the cheek as we walked, held tightly and smiled while looking straight ahead. Disarmed completely, I, too, kept eyes ahead.

On entering the courtyard to my apartment building, Joan noticed that the plastic bag I was carrying was leaking. Something inside had burst open. The toddler was delighted, screaming at her own echo, so I gave Joan my keys and she went on with the child up to my apartment.

I put the bag on the ground and reached to the bottom and produced a leaking yogurt tub, extra large size. While Avril transferred and re-arranged the groceries, I walked it at arm's length to the dustbin enclosure at one end of the yard. I was about to discard it in a tall metal bin when Avril looked up.

"No, don't," she said, concerned. She left the groceries and approached. "It's more than half full." She took it from my hand, peeled back the lid and carefully licked it. The strong evening light shone on her face when she tilted back her head.

She closed her eyes and drank. The outside of the cracked container was coated with the thick white liquid, but she held it firmly. The yogurt oozed between her fingers. I watched her swallow. I almost felt it slide down her throat. I wanted my hands to slide about the curves of her body as smoothly. I wanted her sticky fingers to spread and press into my body. She opened her eyes to look at me before she took the container away from her mouth. Smiling contentedly, she licked her fingers then wiped her lips with one index finger as she offered the yogurt to me to drink.

"We shouldn't waste it," she said quietly, aware that perhaps we were under observation, but determined to finish the container where we stood.

"Right," I replied, almost hypnotized by her. I swallowed some. She finished it without hesitation, discarded the empty container in the nearest tall bin and crossed the yard to retrieve the groceries. How sensuous she was. How practical.

Avril was never shy. I have never seen her embarrassed. This I have always admired in her. When we were children attending national school, Avril used to lead several of her friends, including myself, on forays to the various embassies on Ailesbury Road and about town, the purpose of which was to gather as many glossy brochures as was possible on the pretext of doing a school project.

"Is the ambassador in?" she would ask. "Well then, we want some information about your country," she would say when told that the ambassador would not be able to see us. If we couldn't have the ambassador they would have to give us a consolation prize.

☆   ☆   ☆   ☆

Joan soon left with the toddler to rendezvous with her babysitter friend and collect her two neighbours.

"Why didn't you tell us before?" Avril asked me when we were alone. "Honestly, you're so childish," she said as though speaking to a child. She went into the bedroom to change her clothes. I did not follow. Instead, I opened my door to the landing and sat down on the top step of the staircase, intent on having a rhetorical conversation with myself. I knew there was a rich sound to be had in that plain, dark shaft. I spoke loudly, louder than was necessary for Avril to hear. I enjoyed the knowledge that my neighbours would hear also (although most of them were old and did not speak English). I kept my eyes on the view of the far side of the courtyard framed in the landing window below.

"You can't just go round advertising your birthday. *I* can't do it." Terry 'me' was very much to the point. Terry 'the other' was, naturally, understanding and sympathetic; polite, too. "I mean, what was I supposed to do? Wear a T-shirt with IT'S TERRY'S BIRTHDAY ON MONDAY on it? Well, it looks that way. Oh, it's too late now. Next year, then. Big letters on the front: TERRY – HATCHEL'S – BIRTHDAY – THIS – MONDAY. Bright colours would help. Right, bright colours. I could have it on the back, too, and perhaps a graphic – a birthday cake. *Your* birthday cake. Right, *my* birthday cake. Chocolate. Very nice." I heard Avril come to the door. Without turning, I sensed her attractiveness; the alluring presence that bridged the space behind me. I kept my eyes on the landing window below. She watched me gesticulate. I stood up and sat down like the horn players did in the big swing bands.

"I mean, what was I supposed to do? Just blurt it out? Oh, *I* know! I should have dropped a hint. Of course! I wouldn't have had to say: 'It's *my* birthday on Monday.' I could have dropped a hint. I could have said: 'It's *Terry's* birthday on Monday.' Brilliant! Fucking brilliant!"

"Shhh!" said Avril, trying not to laugh. She grasped my outstretched hands from behind. "You *did* tell us."

"A bit late, though, wasn't it?"

☆   ☆   ☆   ☆

At the dinner Joan put her tongue in my ear. I encouraged her. Bob told the party more than once that he had a dog named Adolf. Joan's neighbours were polite and made intelligent conversation. They recommended that Joan take Avril to Brockburg, a bar exclusively for women, before her holiday ended. They paid Avril much attention, as though she were *their* special guest.

I had to play a late night gig with the band. I told Joan where we were playing, but warned it was a rough place. Each agreed to come to see the band. Bob left with me.

Bob and I met Mac and the band for my birthday drink before we played at what we called 'The Supermarket' – named so because that was what it had been. They had taken the shelves out, painted the place black and installed a long shoddy bar at one end. It was in the Turkish quarter. When we arrived to do a sound check we found a woman covered in pinned money. We had a Turkish wedding for a supporting act.

At 3.00 a.m. when we finished another lousy rendition of our lousy repertoire, Mac said that he and the others had had enough of Berlin and Hamburg and were going home. He asked if I wanted to stay with them. We all went for another drink. It was the last time we were together as a group.

Bob and I went to an all night bar in Kantstrasse. Avril, Joan and her two friends had not arrived at the club by the time we left.

We got thoroughly drunk. Early in the morning the bartender answered the telephone.

"Terry Hatchel," he called, addressing the sparse gathering. "Are you Terry Hatchel?" he asked me in German.

"No, not today," I replied, still drunk.

"Here, give us that. I am," said Bob to the bartender after asking me what the enquiry was. It was Joan on the other end of the line. She knew I had frequented that place since I first came to Berlin. She had guessed we were there. "Get us out of here," Bob said to her. "He's talking about wanting a Turkish wedding. I don't know where we are, just come and get us – and *don't* bring Avril."

God knows what I had said to Bob in my drunken stupor.

☆   ☆   ☆   ☆

For the week and a half Bob endured being fugitive it seemed he and I lived on vitamin pills and coffee; bright orange pills, black, black coffee. During the day I volunteered numerous unimportant lies about myself, compounding and supplementing unimportant lies I had written on postcards. Bob came shoplifting with me. I had stopped off in Holland to shoplift. I had done it in Hamburg. I did it in Berlin. Bob knew I had stolen from shelves since childhood. I had told him I would do it even when I was famous. He didn't shoplift, he said, because it was more fun to watch. My tours and explanations for Bob and Avril's benefit were at best vague, more often pointless. What did it matter? Being together was what was important.

We explored the distractions, advantages and cost of living in a twenty-four hour city, often, to my regret, at Avril and Joan's expense. Their tolerance of us went unrewarded.

"Dublin can be twenty-four hours if you know the ropes," Bob told me. "Known to the select few – the Green Rooms in certain theatres – they're some of the best places."

I told him to close his eyes and count to ten; we were not in Dublin.

We didn't get enough sleep. We drank too much. Most nights we slept in Joan's flat because, as Bob put it, the electricity was better in her house.

Anything could have happened. There were so many options. No one of us knew the extent of our freedom, or what each of us wanted. We played hard; solicited each others' attention with what we thought funny because it was most revealing.

Every night I slept with Avril I gave her all that was in me, just as I give my breath to the conical tube with valves that are the definitive ifs and buts of that shining contortionist which opens to a bell and makes my breath my voice: a voice more lucid than my own, made so by my fingers.

When I woke in the morning after the first night we were alone, Avril was turned away, asleep, but she lay close to me. I felt she was still gently sucking my tongue into her mouth and I was still wedged in the warmest part of her body. Her hair I clutched between the fingers of my hand, but not taut. I lay there for a while without moving. I lifted and let fall the strands. I weighed her hair between my spread fingers. It was a moment of peace she would not know she had given to me. It was the thank you she would not hear.

☆   ☆   ☆   ☆

Avril's remarks about Joan and me were tortuous and amusing, the fruit of homework done thoroughly by a confident and resourceful tactician. They say that if interrogated, the best response is to tell truthfully *everything* you know, thus placing your captors in the uncomfortable position of being unsure whether or not you are to be believed. With this in mind, I told her I had not slept with Joan; that of course I found her attractive; that when I arrived in Berlin I had the names of two club owners and her telephone number and that I recognized the danger of thinking she was the only person in the city and on this I had based my principle that we were friends, exiles in the same city. Would I compromise my principles? Under certain circumstances, yes, I would, and not just my own, but such circumstances had not arisen.

"I understand," Avril said, draining every drop of credibility out of the truth. I was exasperated.

She took from her hair the bulldog clip which gathered the heavy strands, and shook her head gently once. She moved towards Bob seductively and pressed her body to his.

"Let's dance, Bob," she said, pushing his hands around her waist, her eyes examining, her breath following her gaze. She held him tightly. She pressed the lower part of her body into his. She moved in slow dance steps, taking him with her. She put her head on his shoulder and continued her attack.

" . . . you see, Terry, Bob only needs one woman."

My defence was unco-ordinated. I threw out phrases and short sentences that were mildly abusive, wholly ineffective. I could not stand still. I made exaggerated 'Hah' sounds to exhibit my disbelief and dramatize my role of victim. She lifted her head from Bob's shoulder and slid her hands around to his stomach and up to the collar of his shirt. Seven buttons not counting the spare. She started from the top. Slowly, she undid each one. She pulled the front flaps out of his trousers to undo the seventh. Bob was swaying instead of breathing. She took his shirt off and let it fall to the floor.

"Terry, you don't mind me dancing with your best friend, do you?" she asked looking at Bob's chest.

"Dis-gusting!" I replied, peeved. "Don't *you* mind her, Bob."

She had her back to me but I could tell she reached for his trousers button by watching her elbows.

"Don't stand there, Bob!" I protested.

She said something to him in a low voice: "Don't worry. I won't go any further," I think it was. To emphasize my presence I moved to watch them in profile. Her firm breasts seemed to strain towards him. I felt weak. She pressed her fingers into his back and pulled herself to him and continued to dance slowly. He said nothing. He just swayed whatever direction she took him.

When the morning light broke, Bob panicked and left for London where he got drunk with Pete before returning to Dublin.

Chapter 9

POISON THE BABYSITTER

JOAN AND Avril decided to visit Brockburg.

The toddler had been put to bed for the second time and all was quiet. Joan and Avril had waited for half an hour to ensure that she was asleep. I told them not to wait any longer; she couldn't but be asleep after half an hour's silence. (You see how quickly you can become expert in these matters.)

They had a conscience about leaving me, a not able body, with no one but the child. Would I be able to cope if I had to change a nappy, for she would not let me rest until it was changed? Of course I would. I told them to get out and give me a full report over breakfast.

They stood in the doorway and said good-bye softly so as not to wake my charge. Was it me being sick that made Joan and Avril seem more alluring than I had ever seen either of them?

I lay on my mattress trying to decide how ill I was. I ached. I was sweating. My taut stomach was probing for a way out. I determined to lie absolutely still. This I was not destined to do, however. The toddler came running out of her cave and stopped and stood in the middle of the floor looking at me. I raised my head to look, and waited what I feared was the three beats toddlers allow before crying after a fall or deprivation of some kind. I braced myself. Nothing happened. I offered a token "Hello". Nothing happened. The gods had granted a further delay because of my condition. Suddenly, I felt confident. I would speak to the toddler. I told her that Joan and Avril had gone to a feminist bar in which I would not be welcome. I explained that I was unwell: food poisoning, I had at first thought, but now blamed the water. I asked if there was anything she wanted: a cigar, perhaps, or the newspapers? Had she done anything? (Joan's words about her not letting me rest until I had changed her nappy echoed in my head so I concluded, owing to the silence, she had not.) She seemed slightly curious, strangely content. I feared an outburst was imminent.

"You don't want to go to bed yet, do you?" I said, nodding to indicate that I knew she did not. "Do you want to play?"

I had expected she might tumble onto my mattress, but she did not move. Then I had a bright idea. I must have been crazy with fever.

"Let's make some music," I said, throwing back the eider-down and getting to my feet.

It seemed to take forever to pick out all the notes. I leaned in the door-frame between living room and hall, my head light, my legs weak, my forehead, hands and back sweating as I gently pumped out 'Teddy Bears' Picnic'.

The toddler loved it. She squeaked, stamped over to me and looked for the notes coming out of the sax. She then went to my mattress, crash-dived and with a gurgling sound, to my amazement, fell asleep. I debated whether I should sleep in a chair or take a chance on moving the toddler so as to allow me room to lie down. I dare not have moved her to her own room. I got violently sick in the bathroom before making any decision.

I decided to make room beside her, but before lying down I thought it wise to pin a note on the toddler's door in case Joan had a fit when she saw the abandoned cot:

BABY A 1
(I drew an arrow)
☆ ☆ ☆ ☆

Avril watched me through the window of the Chinese hand laundry. I was respectfully arguing with the elderly proprietor over a missing button. It became apparent that I would have to accept the old man's polite but firm refusal to be held responsible for the loss of the button. I paid the amount due but felt some kind of protest was in order (something that he would respond to – I had never complained to a Chinaman before and he was making it difficult for me to consider any kind of threat. It would have to be something that would impress Avril.) I delayed until another customer entered the laundry, then I changed my shirt where I stood. I could not decide whether or not the proprietor was embarrassed. He was uncomfortable, of that I am sure. Avril *was* impressed. I rolled the shirt I had been wearing into a tight ball, took an exaggerated bow and left with dignity.

Outside, I stopped in the doorway to light a cigarette.

"Just as well I didn't leave my shiny metallic-blue mohair suit in for cleaning," I said, trying to push my thumb through an unemployed button hole.

"Have you got a mohair suit?" Avril asked with sudden interest.

"Not yet," I replied. "I will have."

"So you're missing a button," she said, disappointed. She plunged two fingers into my breast pocket in search of the button. "Have you checked in here?"

"No," I replied. "Other people's shirts have a spare button, but *my* shirt has a spare button hole."

"Buy a new shirt!" said Avril. "I saw some beautiful shirts on Kurfürstendamm."

"Euro-man clothes," I said dismissively. "Have you any idea how much a new shirt would cost here?" I asked. "I'm fussy."

She parted my shirt where the button was missing and peered in at my chest.

"Mm, I can see why you're fussy," she said. "I could show you how to sew a button on."

I handed her the shirt I had rolled up into a ball. That is

the nearest I have ever been to being married. I felt as the proprietor of the laundry had felt when I changed my shirt in his shop.

What did Avril want to get married for?

She could have stayed longer with me in Berlin if she had wanted. At the airport I sat with her in the bar wondering how I had frightened her away. That morning I was so nervous we left for the airport two hours too early.

Did you ever find yourself walking behind a woman late at night down a quiet street and you realize that she's aware of you so you pick up speed in order to pass her out so she doesn't think you are following her? Then she starts walking faster as you approach – now she really thinks you are after her – so you shift into top gear. That's when she glances round and breaks into a run.

☆   ☆   ☆   ☆

"You don't know how to accept anything offered," said Avril. "You're not too good at giving, either – I mean, nobody gets a look in at you. It's all a big bloody secret."

"I like being under suspicion," I replied.

"Nobody satisfies you; you're so damn self-centred."

"Oh yeah?" I said wearily.

"The only thing you're serious about is your own success." She began to soften. She had been wanting to say all this for a long time because she cared about me. "I know you're talented, but you must allow people into your life."

"You tell them all in Dublin I'm living on my own," I said.

After her plane had departed I went to the bar in Kantstrasse. I got drunk to show her how serious and how talented I was.

LIGHT BLUE TOUCH PAPER AND RETIRE is the instruction on fireworks. This is what she had done to me.

When I returned to my apartment there was a message from Avril on the telephone answering machine. She had rung from Dublin airport to say that she was sorry and that I was to ignore what she had said, that she was drunk and in a nasty mood when she said it. I was still quite drunk myself when I rang her to say that it didn't matter, that I was sorry for ignoring what she had said.

"You see!" she said exasperated, "You don't know how to accept a bloody thing."

She was extremely annoyed with me for not allowing her to apologize and said that I couldn't go on excluding others in such a way. I told her I was drunk and asked her who the hell did she think she was. She thought I was being flippant.

☆   ☆   ☆   ☆

A week after Avril left I got a telephone call from Ulli Toller. Otto Rollig had contacted him. He had a teenage girl vocalist named Bretta cutting an LP and he wanted me to blow sax.

All the session musicians played their parts well; sight read fast; made no mistakes. The background vocalists were always in harmony, in spite of being paid only 130 DM per track and 50 DM extra for each one overdubbed. However, the LP was worthless, but the girl was attractive, so Otto Rollig put her on television and had her lip sync. to the recording.

Subsequently, I got more work in Hamburg. A lot of it was playing from complicated music sheets – 'fly shit' we call it. None of it moved me, or any of the other musicians. Call it 'fly shit' but don't laugh at it; play it. That is the rule.

I had to hitch to Hamburg (I would not be paid for work on the Bretta LP for two months – it is not uncommon for studios to delay payment to accumulate interest). I had trouble on my return to Berlin. At the border with the DDR the West German police pointed out that my three month visa had expired. In Berlin I would have to fill out forms and get 'angemeldet'.

As soon as I returned to the city Otto Rollig asked me to play in the backing group for Bretta's live performance. I agreed. I wished I hadn't.

There was a large audience. I didn't know why. Joan and her boyfriend were present. Mac, too. He had come to say good-bye. He had the train tickets in his pocket. He and the band had stayed in Berlin as long as they could, waiting for something to come of the demo tapes.

He watched from the wings. I made a point of not wanting music sheets. I was ashamed to be part of the act.

"What the fuck is 'angemeldet'?" I asked him after the performance.

"I don't know," he said, "a visa of some sort. I don't care either, as long as you don't need it to get out of here."

I saw them off at the Zoo Station. They were going back to what they had come from and the fools were in high spirits hanging out of the coach windows.

"See ya in Dublin, head!" Mac shouted.

☆   ☆   ☆   ☆

Joan explained to me that angemeldet meant I had to find a guarantor, an employed resident of Berlin.

"Normally, at this stage there is a German girlfriend," an American musician told me in Joe's Bierhaus. "A nurse or a primary school teacher. She loves musicians and follows you everywhere. When angemeldet comes up she suggests you marry her."

I went to the police station in Charlottenburg and stood in a long queue waiting for them to mispronounce my name over the intercom, watching others in the queue picking at their feet.

I had the whole thing organized when it happened – I became what I am now: better off by far. I got a chance to play sax with the big boys. The band had come from England. Their tour included a concert at Deutschlandhalle and their own sax player had fallen sick and fallen from favour simultaneously. I travelled with them. The tour finished in London. Early in my life I had learned to pursue offers of work diligently, but to get excited only at the beat before I blow the first note. I got what assurances of work I could get before leaving London for a short time. I returned to Dublin and found that I was in the uncomfortable position of being the only person who knew me that had doubts about my ability to be a respected, well-paid, professional musician. No one checked for damage to or improvement of my ear, my breath, my fingers.

When I went back to London the band manager put me on a retainer. It was the first time I had a musician's weekly income, ironically, not for performing. It was not a lot: a talented busker's weekly takings; enough to make me worry about having to busk for ever and a day.

I toured the United States and Canada with the band, a tour that was not a success. I returned to London and became a resident of near the middle, blowing sax with some of the finest musicians alive. It is because of my ability that I play with them and they with me. I avoid entertaining the notion that luck or circumstance are, in part, responsible because it does not matter now. When *nothing* matters at the moment but what you play, you are playing with the best. When playing with the best there exists a secret told only in the completed music.

Chapter 10

SEVEN SONGS

W E HAD set up. Mac and Larry were tuning.
I was cursing Bob again over the bent key. Mrs O'Connor had
entered the room alone and was standing close to me.

"A bad workman always blames his tools," she said teasingly as I carefully bent the key back into place.

"So do people with faulty tools," I replied. Secretly, she
took keen delight in my curtness.

"Can you make music?" Rosie asked me, pointing her
microphone at me.

"You bet!"

Mrs O'Connor took this as her notice to usher in the
guests.

Rosie had developed hiccups, caused possibly by nerves,
more likely by the wine. I got her a glass of water from the
kitchen. When I returned I found Avril and her husband had
slipped away from the crowd to be first in the room and offer
their appreciation. They were chatting to Rosie. Avril was
amused by Rosie's hiccups.

Rosie blocked her ears by applying pressure with her
fingers. I held the glass to her mouth. She drank. I tipped the
glass forward as she tilted her head back. She swallowed all of
the water, keeping her ears blocked. Avril laughed, but she

stopped when I looked expressionless at her.

"An old stage trick, I suppose?" asked her husband lightly.

"I panic at the prospect of a nose bleed," I said sharply. "Most performers do." They knew I was not being funny. "O.K., Rosie?"

"Yes, I'm ready," she said smiling. Her hiccups had gone. Other people were being ushered in by Mrs O'Connor. I put the glass down and took up my saxophone. It made clear to Avril I did not want to talk with her at that moment.

We opened with two Leiber/Stoller numbers The Coasters made classics: 'Along Came Jones' and 'Yakety Yak'. Rosie ripped through the lyrics. The band was tight. The sharp notes I pumped I shot through the breaks between verses. Rosie then sang 'True Love Ways', a Buddy Holly number, gentle and lingering with a soft counter melody for which I dearly wished I had my tenor sax. Patrick accompanied on clarinet. 'He's a Rebel' followed, a Pitney number The Crystals made a classic. I blew underneath. Rosie sang out at the audience like the rebel's girl should. The band stayed tight. Larry then awkwardly adjusted a microphone and mumbled. The band played. Larry sang 'Ya Ya' with his chin on his chest so that the lyrics rolled on the roof of his mouth. Rosie and I had no part in this one. Rosie then announced that I would sing. I just did it; I hated doing it, particularly in front of Avril because it showed me at less than my best, but I did not hesitate. I borrowed Mac's acoustic guitar which he had not used in the set, briefed the others and pulled the microphone to my mouth.

"This one is for Avril," I said with what must have sounded like little conviction; it was nervousness. "Of course, they're all for Avril," I added with even more uncertainty, "and what's-his-name." I stepped back a foot from the ambiguous reaction, tuned quickly, had one false start, then played and sang Eddie Cochran's 'Three Steps to Heaven'.

Rosie completed the set with a song she wrote herself called 'My Daddy Said He Used to Look Like Elvis'. I had not heard it before. I decided I would scarcely render a sax presence and let Patrick trace her voice on the clarinet. This was not to be, however, because he stayed at the piano. Perhaps you could describe it as an up-tempo blues number. It crept under my skin and pressed on my lungs, composing the breath that I made notes of.

For this last song she finally won the admiration of the whole gathering.

We had performed; we had finished. I had successfully avoided conversation with Avril until now. I knew that to speak to her would be like trying to sing with a mouthful of water. Even with my dark glasses on, not once had I glanced at her during the seven songs, in spite of her positioning herself so that it would be hard for me not to see her. I had kept her at bay. I don't recall having played better before or since.

Chapter 11

PLAYING TO THE SEPTICS

AVRIL INTRODUCED me to her husband, John. John and Avril, John on Avril, John in Avril, Avril on John, Avril and John. He shook hands vigorously like Mr O'Connor did.

"Pleased to meet you, Terry," he said with an insurance salesman's smile. I smiled thinly in return.

"I saw you at the church," I said. He was not amused by what he thought was a joke, but his grin broadened. "From a distance you look like a marriage guidance counsellor. Even from this distance," I added. "Everything should be fine," I said turning to Avril. She laughed nervously as if to warn me to go no further. He was unsure how to react to my ambiguous delivery of a derisive remark. He was not dull-witted. He was quick to take offence.

"You're the one who sent us the money, aren't you? We can't take it, of course."

"It wasn't me, sir. I was not the one. I just came with Bob and Albert." This annoyed him.

"Well, we don't think it's appropriate," he said.

"We *do* appreciate it," Avril said, intervening anxiously.

"Yes," I said replying to him, "they've been a bad influence. Even now I have had to send them off."

"No, the money." He was now angry. At that point he was called away to another group by an insistent friend. "Excuse me," he said with a twitch of his head, looking at me first, then Avril. "I'll be back shortly." With that promise, he left us alone.

"You are *so* insulting!" said Avril, disgusted with me.

"He's quite sharp," I continued. "I thought he might be a bit retarded – his nails are cut back severely – but no ... "

"Terry, I don't mind you being funny, but don't spoil my day."

"I almost turned up too late," I said as though it were a belated threat.

"I'm so glad you're here. You were wonderful. Thank you."

"That was Rosie singing."

"You really look the part, don't you?" she said admiringly.

"What, a funny man?"

"No! Rock star. Don't be smart."

"I told you, people like Rosie are the stars. I'm a musician – a good one – and quite presentable. I play timely solos for a lot of money. I'm number one punctuator."

"That's what you wanted."

"You bet."

"I knew it would work out for you. We're all so proud of you."

"We?"

"Your friends. The 'scruffier element'," she said smiling, "I *am* your friend?"

"Yeah, well don't expect much from a jealous man."

"You've no idea how much I appreciate that, Terry," she said sincerely, almost lovingly. She then deliberately changed to a lighter tone. "Bob's such a character! He and Albert should have stayed. I don't mind who they offended. You shouldn't have let them go. He must have been very drunk when he made his speech! And you! You encouraged him. You're as bad as he is!"

"We were just thinking alike."

"Poor fellow. Not everyone appreciates Bob's sense of humour. I love it!"

"He's a funny man, alright. He froze your mother's gold-fish in the deep freeze." She didn't notice I wasn't being funny.

"I couldn't help laughing when I heard 'where's moh horse?' It's been a while since we've all been to the pictures together. Although, when Bob stood up in the middle of it all and started, it was like being *in* a film."

"Well, I like films with action. Bob certainly provided some of that." I nodded to Avril's husband standing among a group of his friends. "I've been watching," I said. "Except to dance, he hasn't touched you once. I don't like films in which nobody touches." It must have sounded very sour. "What the hell did you marry him for? Because there was nothing else to do? Because it's time to *settle down*? In Berlin I meant . . . I never talked about looking for someone because I just wanted you in my life. I thought you'd know I . . . " I did not finish the sentence. I checked myself; said: remember, you're not there with her, you're here at her wedding; you're visiting home; you live in London; you've got a recording session in Soho next week – Tuesday morning, 9.30am.; rock 'n' roll with the big boys; it will be a great record – a classic; then, the tour of the States – "playing to the septics," as the band's cockney roadies describe it, septics being short for septic tanks, being cockney rhyming slang for yanks.

"I'll never forget the time we spent together in Berlin," she said. "I know you think I have. You're special to me . . . "

"Stop," I said in a low, even voice. "It just stops. I haven't come from Berlin."

She muttered discontentedly and took my glasses off.

"Did you think I wasn't paying attention?" I asked as she fingered the frames.

"Still can't get through to you," she said.

"What a thing to happen to you," I replied. She had to remove the glasses from in front of my eyes because words were as useful to me as a wet cardboard box.

"You shouldn't have sent us that money, Terry." She was

looking me straight in the eyes.

"Special privilege. It's not for him," I said looking away. They were both lines from my prepared script.

Mrs O'Connor interrupted and held her daughter by the arm. She asked my body if she might borrow Avril. I saw her in a post office window looking out at me as she licked an envelope.

"Take her," I said.

"Can you look after yourself – just for a minute?" Avril asked. I nodded 'yes'. "Are you sure?" she said kindly; she was telling me she wanted to finish our conversation.

"Yes," I said. "You ask anybody," I said pointing at random with my chin.

Mrs O'Connor took her daughter away. I stood for a moment posing. I turned my attention to Avril's husband and his group standing in a crescent-shaped Terry trap. I stared at him; willed him over to me. The same twitch of his head as he said 'excuse me'. Maybe he thought I had insulted Avril, his wife.

"Would you care to join them – the merry little group?" he said tiredly. "Before you say yes, I'd advise against it. Boring old farts the lot of them and they are no older than me. Let's you and me have a drink."

I was very suprised by his attitude towards his friends and his change of attitude towards me. For the second time that day I had underestimated how much someone had drunk.

He insisted on wandering, but kept his pace to mine. We ended up in the kitchen where others passed through but did not stay among the mountains of messed dishes and half consumed food and drink.

"When did it happen, John?" I asked. "When did you ask Avril to marry you?"

"Pardon?"

"You were on a bus. She kept yawning at you so to stop her you leaned over and said: 'Excuse me, would you marry me please?' "

"Look here!" he retorted.

"Stopped her yawning, but she said yes."

"You've made it quite clear I'm not popular with you and your friends," he said matter-of-factly, then drained his glass. "What *is* going on, Terry? I can't help feeling I've been a bad boy. It's *my* wedding. I'm not supposed to feel like that. Avril is not at ease thanks to you and Bob and the other fellow."

He was disconcerted by my retrieving from the deep freeze the now solid state goldfish kit. I held it in front of my face for close inspection. I dictated where or at whom the fish looked by rotating the bowl. I made it stare at him.

"We just might turn up looking for dinner one day," I said. "If we do, you better let us in."

"Do you know," he said looking around the bowl, "I like you, Terry," he declared as though it should come as a big surprise. It did. "I know Avril does, too ... " I wanted to hit him. " ... To answer your question," he continued, having regained the confidence the fish had robbed him of, "when I asked Avril to marry me she was wearing a bath towel, nothing else. I asked her if she'd get married in the same dress!" He laughed.

"That isn't funny," I said, lowering the bowl so our eyes met.

"I love that jacket," he declared, as though it were responsible for distracting him from his attempts at being outrageous.

"Do you? Anybody can get one. Fifty quid on the Kings Road." I put the bowl down on the counter. "Here," I said emptying the pockets, "it's yours," I said pulling my jacket off and throwing it at him. "Put it on."

He put it on as a dare. I picked up the goldfish bowl and tossed it to him as his hands came through the sleeves. He caught it, but it was heavy and he let it drop out of fright. The glass shattered on the floor and the ice broke into large pieces. The goldfish, suspended in one, went skating under the table. John laughed louder than before. I left him standing. I wanted out of there fast. I searched the crowd for Rosie.

"Are you ready, Rosie?" I asked her immediately we met.

"Yes, we've packed the gear. Hadn't you better say good-bye to Avril?"

"Right."

"You find her. I'll be over in a minute."

Avril was looking for her husband, or perhaps me.

"I'm not drinking now," I said to her. "I'd make a fool of myself if I did . . . I gave my jacket to your boyfriend. See, over there. Blue mohair."

I had sent her a wad of bank notes in the post in a brown envelope for a wedding present. I didn't write a covering letter, just: 'Best wishes, Terry' on the top bank note.

Madness? I didn't send a cheque because I thought she would not have cashed it. I sent money because it was easy for me. It was impersonal; I liked that. I didn't have to think about *their* needs and wants.

Now, I thought about my coldness towards her as she stood in front of me lightly brushing her lips with her fingertips, momentarily engrossed in the memory of some intimacy. Her kiss was brief, but she held tighter than she ever did before.

Chapter 12

FUNNY MAN

"WHY DON'T you leave, Rosie?" I asked in the taxi on the way to Bob's studio. "Come to London. You should be past saying 'please mister, can we play at your garden party?' " I was angry because whe was not.

"You know I've already been, Terry. Larry isn't ready to go and I need more time with the band."

"This time we'll make sure you go to the right people. On your own, if necessary. Larry is a good guy, but he doesn't shine as a musician. Leave him."

"And go with you?" she asked with a wry smile. She did not take exception to what I had said, nor was she shocked I had said it.

"On your own," I repeated.

"I'm selfish enough to think about it," she assured me.

"What's being selfish? Eating is being selfish? You're more than ready. Those numbers we did back there – you sung all of them magnificently, in spite of the backing."

"They never played better. We've been working well together."

"You sung your own song the best. Rosie, what are you doing? A couple of Saturday night cabaret gigs at fifty or sixty quid a go – most of those resident bands you have to play with are so fuckin' terrible they give you the old three chord trick so you have to sing them all in the one key. I know the punters love it, but just because it's better to have a good singer and a bad band than the other way round."

"Larry says he's not going to play much longer," said Rosie. "Two weeks ago he and the boys were playing a gig in one of those sprawling suburban pubs and when they didn't play the national anthem at the end of the night Larry got beaten up. He's going to try to manage us he says. Maybe he too thinks he's not such a hot musician after all."

I shook my head and clenched my teeth. I rested my head on the back of the seat. She knew I was angered. She also knew I was aware of my harsh words I did not regret having said.

Rosie was looking out of the car window, allowing the passing street lights to track across her face at regular intervals. She turned to me.

"Well, whatever about the others, when it's time, when I get the big chance, *I'll* be ready."

How serious she was I could not ascertain. She had spoken with remarkable ease and with a note of irony. I looked at her for a moment. She winked slowly, deliberately. God, she's so professional!

"That chef," she said after a long pause.

"What chef?"

"The one catering at the O'Connor's. He's a singing chef."

"Oh Christ, you should have told me," I said. "We could have got him to do a number. He could have joined the band."

"He sings cabaret down in Tramore on his holidays," she said beginning to laugh. She had anticipated my response perfectly. I had to laugh with her.

☆   ☆   ☆   ☆

Bob's studio is funded by the Arts Council. He shares it with three other artists. It is a mews in an area of Dublin built in the Victorian era. The previous occupants had done much of the unique decoration themselves. They were artists who had lived and prospered in a world of their own making which involved what seemed to have been a secret network of friends and buyers you could only imagine as being like them. In leaving for an extended stay in sunny foreign parts they left on a short lease basis their converted coach house in the hands of the Arts Council with the proviso that it be used for the purpose it now purported to be put to. This unprecedented, informal offer became a formal but vague arrangement between artists and Council; a source of slight embarrassment owing to that vagueness generated by the benefactors, and, for the moment, a source of good fortune.

I was pleased to find no changes had been made to the living room. When I first saw the place I was utterly taken by its atmosphere – its uniqueness, privacy and durable comfort.

"It's the way the furniture is," Bob had said. Now it was a hideaway I was glad to run to; a place I could borrow in which I thought I might quieten.

It was as I remembered it when I last was in it. Upstairs were the living quarters. Pink, gold, yellow, wine, green and brown. Those were the colours; all rich, or dark, or faded. The living room was pleasantly dark, making the restricted light from the three windows, which were browed by roofing and branches, all the brighter. Most of the furniture was dark and heavy and was on dull brass wheels or curving ball-and-claw legs. The upholstery had faded before the furniture had been placed in this room.

The kitchen area beside the stairwell was open to the living room and was lit in daytime by a small skylight and what light could be trapped from the living room. The gas stove, once white, was now the yellow of old paperbacks and yet appeared to be the brightest of the solid objects of both rooms.

The curtains were heavy, too long for the windows they served (the finest second-hand curtains I have seen) with lavish pelmets. The walls were covered with silk damask, pink in colour, such as I have never seen in clothing. A rich, dull pink seemingly derived from a crimson, with light catching the threads of a subtle organic pattern. The plain but stained carpet was an approximate of the same pink, the dominant colour in the living room.

In contrast to the extravagance of silk damask was the beading, the border between wall and ceiling. Hard wood painted with gold leaf it appeared to be, but was, in fact, polystyrene with gold pigment. The old men had been skilful and clever in matching the opulence of the past – which must have been a legacy or gift of some kind, for undoubtedly they had hung the damask themselves – with the severe financial restrictions of their world.

In the chamber that connected living room with bedrooms and bathroom (it could scarcely be called a corridor or passage), on the brighter pink wallpaper darker broad pink stripes had been hand-painted by the elderly artists. The hot press was housed in this chamber. The gurgles of the immersion heater could be heard in bedrooms, bathroom, living room and kitchen.

The small, oddly proportioned bathroom had a skylight set in its slanting roof, providing a key source of light for the illumination of an intricate collage applied directly to the partition wall furthest from the plumbing, nearest the hot press which ensured that it would stay dry. Among and set against the newsprint, coloured paper and picture material, were superbly executed miniature oil paintings of naked figures.

The two bedrooms had been sealed. The keyholes had tear-shaped brass flaps.

Downstairs was in complete contrast. It was not lived in. One of the rooms was used for general storage. Another, smaller, had been converted into a photographic darkroom with unlabelled brown and green bottles of chemicals and old equipment which had not been used for some time. The two remaining rooms were studios, the largest of which housed a full-sized easel and a number of canvases finished and unfinished, some painted on both sides, packed in crates. The four ground floor rooms and hallway were sparsely furnished, had no decoration, and only bare concrete floors. The two old men had priorities when spending their money. So had Bob.

"I have to do the walls down here," he had said to me. "I'm waiting on a tin of stolen paint."

In a corner of the second studio I saw what I thought was a small pile of black kippers. It was two pairs of policeman's motorbike gauntlets.

☆   ☆   ☆   ☆

Because of the state's official involvement in the studio Bob and his fellow artists feel obliged to hold a board meeting every Friday night. Bob is not the politician or the diplomat of the group. He most certainly is not the treasurer. This is fortunate for the others.

In spite of what had happened at the reception, Bob called the Friday meeting to order because he wanted to contest the officialness of their venture, namely, the need to be registered as a company.

"We're a charity," he declared emphatically. Bob is a surprisingly effective orator when drunk. He produced from his pocket a letter from the tax office. "This letter is addressed to the *Acting Precedent Officer. Acting* Precedent Officer!" he said, with a broad sweep of his hand that almost cost him his balance. "Acting Precedent *Officer!*" he said, leaning forward to fathom the reaction to his phrasing. There was no reaction from the floor. "They were looking for *our* Acting Precedent Officer. That's what you get through the letter-box when they're after ya – when you're a bloody company. I *told* you we shouldn't have registered as a company."

"Yes," said Gerry, the most intelligent of the four, "but I told *you* we *had* to become a company to get the Arts Council grant."

"So *you're* the Acting Precedent Officer!" said Bob with eyes wide open. He handed the letter to Gerry.

"No, I'm not," replied Gerry impatiently. "It's done now. We *are* a registered company. We can't claim rebates on sales of prints, but we *can* write off a lot of tax against capital investment – on the press and the like."

Bob pointed to the window in the envelope.

"You *can't* please these fellas," he said painfully. "They've *got* us unless we un-register. I'd ring them up right now only I can't find the phone book. Albert, ya fucker, have you taken our phone book?"

"But we *can't* just . . . un-register," replied Gerry.

"But we can."

"How do you suggest we do it?"

"Write them a letter saying: Look, we're *terribly* sorry but we've vanished off the face of the earth."

Gerry raised his eyes to the ceiling. "We *are* at this moment registered. We can't just ignore the letter." Gerry pointed to Frank. "Frank understands."

Frank, paralyzed by alcohol, was incapable of confirming or denying anything. Gerry pointed to Dave. "Dave understands."

Dave said that it was the first he had heard of the offensive letter. "Albert understands," said Gerry.

Albert, who is not a member of the studio group, grinned and said he felt like a 'stam' (i.e. a storm).

"We haven't sold a lot yet, have we?" said Gerry.

"Those tax fellas are everywhere," replied Bob. "They're looking for the surprise behind the curtains."

"I suppose you think there's a dozen of them checking up on us right now?"

"Look," said Bob, "I don't know how many of them there are – how many children eat baked beans? – I don't know; I just know it's a lot. Those fellas are everywhere."

"Acting Precedent Officers, baked beans – check that you have a plane ticket," I said to myself aloud. "This is all too familiar." Already I could tell what deodorant Bob's phantom meddlers used.

"As part of the company, Bob," Gerry continued, "you *have* to understand that you can't just ignore the letter."

"Yes I can," replied Bob. "I'll refuse to recognize the post."

☆   ☆   ☆   ☆

"Did I tell you what happened to Adolf?" said Bob to me when the evening seemed to break down. "Did I tell you what happened to the suit? I had to bring the lobster back to that thief on my own, you know. Albert there was away," he said nodding to the seat where Albert no longer sat. "There was only Adolf and me. I left it on the roadside. I didn't go near the place." There was a pause, then he gave a short, snorty laugh anticipating his own words with images. "I parked up the road a bit from the pub – remember, where the hedge was, but the pub fella was ready for us this time. He got me by the jacket. I *wore* the bleedin' suit in case I met him so he'd know I was there on business, not looking for trouble. I let him pull the jacket off me. Adolf got him while I started the motor. I saw the two of them tugging on the jacket. Adolf ripped a hole in it before the pub fella got it from him. He threw rocks at me – that's where the dint in the roof of the Mini came from. He threw them at Adolf, too. You know Adolf – he was too fast for him." There was another pause. "Adolf ran circles round him before he was chased under a car. He didn't die for hours. *He* wouldn't, though, would he?" He laughed again as he did before. It was a cruel test of Bob's outer shell in which the inner being, with dislocated joints, rattled. I was moved, but could think of nothing to say to him. I wanted to choke the emotions out of him, but then, I laughed myself and rattled a bit inside, also.

"Who's playing at the Magnet tonight, Rosie?" I asked, hoping Bob would be taken by the idea of going to an old haunt of mine.

"Crazy Cavan and the Rhythm Rockers."

"Hey, we can't miss that! Let's go! It'll be a welcome injection in the head."

Rosie smiled. "Alright." She said nothing more.

"Where are you going?" asked Bob attempting to focus on us as we left.

"We're goin' down duh Magna," I said in the broadest of Dublin accents. " 'Crazy Cavan and the Rhythm Rockers'. Are ya comin'?"

"Ugh! That place is full of dirty hippies," said Bob. "Watch it!"

I ought to have known better. Music to Bob is incidental. He doesn't buy or borrow records, never goes to gigs or concerts, and yet, declares that I am a great musician.

☆　　☆　　☆　　☆

The Magnet is to Dublin what the Cavern was to Liverpool. Apart from the Monday night gigs which are rock 'n' roll and rockabilly, UK rockabilly bands visit occasionally and play on Friday and Saturday nights. The regular Monday night teddy boys turn up in their gear on both nights. They are first there to dance to the records before the live performance. They know all the words and phrasing of all the songs. The requests are the same every week. When the band is on the cramped stage the teds are in full swing. They stand on the seats and slap the plaster beams to the beat – the ceiling is low; the beam over the platform has been chipped by numerous guitars just where MIND YOUR HEAD is scrawled. Heads shake from the hips; cracking quiffs piled high reel on splay-legged dancers wearing crepe-soled shoes with blue suede uppers. Pig tails and dresses imitate the movement of the bodies they serve. Grease, hair-oil and sweat catch the light. There is hard, hard clapping from those standing on the seats around the walls. The drinks rock on the tables. Many in the crowd have fathers who were teddy boys.

In the street, thirty to forty heavy motor bikes were carefully parked in lines. The polished machines belonged to hairy rockers on whom nothing shone. The bow-tied bouncers, the best in town, knew them all just like they knew the teds. Peace would be preserved because everybody agreed that the music was bigger than they were and would break the peace better than they could.

Inside, Crazy Cavan was blowing big engine effects through the p.a. system before ripping into the lyrics of 'My Little Sister's Gotta Motorbike'.

Rosie and I stepped over broken glass on the pavement onto the ill-patterned carpet of the staircase that leads from the street up to the door – a door which, if you arrive late, you half expect will open with a burst and send bouncer, rockers, teds and band manager tumbling backwards down the stairs.

I recognized many of the faces, remembered most of their names. They recognized me, Rosie too. We didn't have to explain we were there for the music. We didn't have to talk a lot because they were there for the music, also. Respect; familiar greetings exaggerated because of the music. In the Magnet I first learned to grasp with ease words from behind music much louder.

A handful of fresh-faced youths dressed in punk clothes and spiky hair entered. The first two paused in the doorway and cheered themselves in with arms raised. One girl, wearing what looked like a piece of Bob's seat cover, a plastic coat and black lipstick, jumped up and down with great enthusiasm. Good humouredly, the teds booed and chanted 'go home'. Encouraged by the reception, the punks bounded into the crowd towards the bar like confident boxers to the ring.

The band played. Rosie and I let the music make instruments of us as it had always done.

When we left the Magnet we got a taxi to Rene's flat, but went via the Royal Hibernian Hotel to collect the percolator.

"Will you stay in Dublin for a few days?" Rosie asked me in the back seat of the car.

"No, I'll go back to London in the morning."

"See you on Top of the Pops, then, or hear you on the radio."

"You bet. Will you come to London soon?"

"Maybe."

"Don't say maybe," I said impatiently. "People *must* choose."

"You mean like Avril choosing to marry that creep instead of living with you?" Her tone was not malicious like mine.

"Yes! And he *is* a creep. I've checked."

"Poor Terry."

"There's always a loser, Rosie. Being the loser is *his* problem. I've learned that."

"You've lost nothing, love," she said, pressing the palm of her hand to my chest. She had a better idea of where my heart was than I. "I'm going home to Larry," she said and kissed me. She got back into the taxi.

"He's a creep, too!" I shouted as it drove away. Adolf

would have gone for the wheels. Rosie looked back and smiled as the taxi turned towards the city.

Rene answered my ring at the door. She looked down at her swollen body. She almost cried. She was happy to see me. I asked her could I stay the night. She liked my oiled hair. She already had a coffee percolator.

☆   ☆   ☆   ☆

Bob had not returned from the studio. He would arrive drunk.

"I had a date with this woman," he would say, "fluent Irish speaker; works in the canteen of the milk board. There's a triumph for ya!" He would conclude that he had spent twenty minutes lost in the 'tropical bushes' on Dun Laoghaire promenade where he had stopped for a pee. It would be some ridiculous story like that.

I couldn't sleep. I wandered about the flat. Rene couldn't sleep, either. We ate apricots from the tin with a fork. From what used to be my flat there was the sound of the constant tearing of paper. It was a sound that, in spite of being low key, once registered could not be ignored.

"Albert the Ripper," I observed dryly. "What *is* he doing? It's four in the morning."

"I don't know," said Rene, "but he's been at it for days now. They're all mad, you know, Terry. I used to think you were, too. What have I let myself in for?" she said, her voice trailing away. She rescued herself. "What was the name of that girl you went to Berlin with?"

"Joan, and I didn't go to Berlin *with* her," I replied, more distracted by the tearing. "I'm going up to see what he's at."

Albert was working on what I could only describe as a 'thing' which was partially suspended from the ceiling. It was an enormous hollow frame made of papier mâché. When I entered, Albert was ripping a telephone directory into shreds. I hardly recognized the place. He had removed almost all the furniture and painted the walls dark, rich colours. There were bowls of a flour and water mixture in various stages of congealment scattered about the floor. There were the remnants of no fewer than twenty telephone directories in addition to seven or eight as yet in solid state. He was chewing lumps of paper as he worked. He had not regained all his faculties.

He showed me a pastel sketch of it.

"Do you recognize her?" he asked. "Gillian. I'm not goin' to call her that, though. They're all Part Twos," he said ceasing to chew for a moment and pointing to the sculpture. "I'm goin' to call her 'Country Life'. Actually, Bob thought of the title."

'I'll bet."

"I'm no model citizen," I said to Rene, "I don't mind tearing a page out of a phone book, but Albert's up there eating them! He got *dozens* of them up there. It's against the law, you know. How can you love your neighbour when he eats telephone directories? He hasn't done any portraits of you, has he? You're right, Rene, him and Bob are getting worse."

"So, aren't you going to tell me about Joan?" she asked.

"Oh, she's an ex-girlfriend. I don't like her anymore. She's got hair like stewed rhubarb."

Rene laughed, but was caught for breath.

"It's no fun having a baby, is it?" I said. She smiled nervously. I sensed she wanted to talk about Bob and her and the baby and what next. I wanted her to talk, but it didn't happen. She was disappointed. I was disappointed. Bob was absent. If it had not been for the fact that she was the only one Bob trusted to look after Adolf while he visited me in Berlin, I would have believed that there was nothing between them but regret.

Bob took the gravel path by storm at 3.30am. At 3.35am. he missed the steps leading to the hall door and fell six feet into the concrete trench in front of the basement window, where he slept until woken by prowling Jimmy. Jimmy did not wait to see what he had stumbled over, but escaped across the front gardens, not without leaving evidence. Bob's body ached but the fall he had suffered caused no damage.

"Just as well clothes dry in the dark, too, eh Jimmy?" he shouted as he clambered out of the trench onto the grass.

Bob slept the rest of the night in the Mini.

☆　　☆　　☆　　☆

When I woke early the following morning I had a taste in my mouth like I had been sucking on a fifty pence piece. It was Rene who woke me. She nudged me gently on the shoulder.

"Get out of the car, Bob!" I shouted. "Jesus Christ, it's an emergency! The fuckin' baby is coming."

Bob was virtually unconcious. I shook him violently. I threw the front seat forward and kicked him. I tried to drag him out, but succeeded only in rolling him onto the floor of the Mini. At that point he awoke and began to resist.

"Je-asus!" I shouted, pushed him back onto the seat and slammed the passenger door. I ran around to the other side and sat in the driver's seat. "Where's the keys, Bob?" I asked employing all my self control. It wasn't funny. "WHERE - ARE - THE - KEYS - BOB?" Bob was curled up on the back seat and had again slipped into that great void you are dispatched to when the telephone number you have dialled fails to connect.

I reached under the dash board and pulled out the ignition appendix. I crossed the wires. The car started. I looked up and saw Rene descending the front steps holding herself together.

"Don't do it," I said. "Get in the car will ya!" I shouted.

I had seen this scene on the television a dozen times. The man is always excited, but gets her to the hospital in time. *He*'s been planning for it for months. I didn't want anything to do with it.

Rene leaned backwards as she got into the Mini. She was gasping. She wasn't saying anything and that wasn't helping me. I was afraid to speak in case it would provoke her. I fumbled for my dark glasses, successfully positioned them on my nose at the second attempt, then looked down between her legs. Nothing had happened yet. I said someting ridiculous like: "Fuckin' hell!" and jammed the gear stick into reverse. The car lurched backwards; into first and it lunged forwards. I pushed the accelerator pedal onto the floor in between changing up the gears.

We roared down the road, Rene about to give birth, the

window rattling in the door panel, Bob in a bundle on the back seat, moaning, and my fly open.

I stopped the car outside the hospital entrance. Rene was no help – she was not fighting it at all. I ran into the building prepared to settle for anyone dressed in white.

"There's a woman out there having a baby," I shouted at the male receptionist. "Do something!"

I was about to leap over the desk and clap an arm-lock on the calm gentleman when two nurses rounded the corner.

"Nurse! Nurse!" I shouted. "Quickly!" They ran to me and we made for the exit. "The car isn't big enough," I said. "It's not hygenic. That bastard, Bob, never cleans it out."

I was ahead of the nurses. I burst through the swing doors to find that Rene had just given birth in the Mini. I made an abortive attempt at throwing up as the nurses tended Rene and the baby. They were anxious. Rene was transfixed. The small crowd that had gathered felt privileged. I felt weak. I sat down on a step. They'll never be able to sell that car now, I thought.

Presently, Bob came alive. Apparently unaware of the drama, he struggled out of the back seat and pissed as high as he could up into the air.

☆   ☆   ☆   ☆

I went to the Royal Hibernian Hotel. I had another look for my tooth-brush. Couldn't find it. Bought a disposable one for 10p from a machine in the men's room. I paid my bill and left the hotel.

I put on my dark glasses and bought some flowers from a hawker in Grafton Street. She wouldn't sell me a dozen red roses – only tens and twenties, she said.

"A dozen red roses is what you're supposed to give your missus," I protested.

"I'm sorry, love," she replied, "I'll give ya twenty for six quid. Tracy, wrap the gentleman twenty red roses."

I paid the taximan who drove me to the airport to deliver the roses to the hospital with a card: FROM BOB TO RENE.

When questioned, Bob, the bastard, would swear he *had* sent them and would believe it himself.

Bob thinks he makes plans, but he doesn't. He can't. Occasionally, he manages to take advantage of a situation and turn what he perceives into a joke or a work of art.

I recall the night I returned from a disastrous provincial trek with an abysmal band. I was dying to smoke every leaf on every plant in the house. I had just decided I would settle for two of Albert's spectacular funnel joints when the drug squad knocked on the door. I had not yet called to Bob or Rene's flat. I had not talked with them.

We had always thought that if there were to be a raid it would have been at dawn. I opened the hall door. There was no mistaking who they were. What betrays plain-clothes policemen is that they all look like they once wore uniforms. They look like badly turned out Mormons and Mormons look like SS officers in plain clothes.

They checked my room, then Bob's and finally Rene's. I was sure I had left something lying around and was shocked when they found nothing. Had I been robbed?

In Bob's room they found Adolf. He had stopped barking. He was saving his energy for an attack. The detective, wanting to be first in each room, half turned the handle to Bob's room then paused. He could hear Adolf sniffing him under the door.

"Does your landlord permit animals?" he asked sharply.

"Ah, he's alright," replied Bob ambiguously.

The detective braved opening the door and, being the first of the strangers attempting to gain entry, duly paid the price. Adolf did not bother to look at the enemy's face; he went straight for the leading leg and tried to drag the giant into his lair. The detective was furious. He kicked Adolf as best he could which, naturally, served only to make Adolf grip tighter on his flannels.

Outside, on the landing, I was feeling weak watching Bob and the mongrel provoke. Before, they might have let us off with a little, but not now. Bob let him bite before intervening. Meanwhile, a second detective searched but found nothing.

There was no strong arm stuff. They were untidy, but they did not wreck our rooms. The detective in charge, the one with sun-burnt ears (he had been to Spain on his holidays) showed me the warrant. In Rene's room he discussed with me the tomato plants Rene kept in pots in the window bay, describing how he had coaxed his last bumper crop. The others searched. They found nothing. There was nothing to find. I was staggered.

Shortly after they left Albert arrived with the best joints I have ever sucked on.

Bob was very pleased with himself as he explained to me what had happened as though he had planned it all. Rene's suspicions had been aroused first. Jimmy had not been round the gardens for nearly two weeks. Either he was sick or had been frightened off or had ceased to pander to his fetish. He wasn't sick, because Rene had seen him holding his mother's hand in the shopping centre. He had not lost interest for he broke away from her to examine covertly some underwear. Therefore, something had frightened him off.

Then Rene realized that the house was being watched. We credited Jimmy with sharp senses. There could be no doubt that if Jimmy thought they were the police, they were, in fact, the police.

Presumably Rene's experience as a research assistant proved useful in thinking of a place to hide our modest supply of drugs, for it was she who suggested temporarily misfiling it in Jimmy's mother's overgrown and disused greenhouse two back gardens away. This Albert and Bob did late one night.

Subsequently, I found Bob at work one day in the art school on a sculpture of what he described as a 'lert'. It was an angular head masterfully carved in apple tree wood. The head was housed in a dog box and would come out when a pole protruding from the far end and geared with springs was pushed. By lifting a trap door the workings could be seen.

"Remember the D. S. detective with the red ears and a jaw like a hoof?" he said pointing to his piece. "Be alert. Ireland needs lerts."

Chapter 13

THE PARROT

I HAD not telephoned my sister. To ring her now from the airport and say I was leaving would be unwise. I did not get to see my niece. She would have to wait for the Mickey Mouse watch. I would telephone her when I got to London and talk to her if my sister allowed her to stay on the line for any length of time.

"You haven't much time for anybody these days," my sister says to me, but I know she is happy for me.

Each time I visit Dublin I find nothing has changed except me, as I am constantly told. They think it should be the same as it used to be when you call and ask them to come out to play. In the past they did not notice that I was less noticeable to those other than them. And yet, at the reception, Rose had privately discredited my conclusions.

"You used to say you'd be famous, Terry," she said.

"Arrogance," I had replied dismissively. I was gratified.

"No, you used to say you were destined to be famous."

"How famous can a saxophonist get?"

Everyone else said: "We knew you'd be famous."

For a long time after we had played, Rosie said nothing. She said little at Bob's studio. I thought she was uncomfortable, that she wanted to be somewhere else, that I shouldn't have told her she deserved better than her lot. Then, just before we entered the Magnet, she stopped me, looked at me, then said she had not realized I was so good. She had said what I had hoped Avril would say when I came to the wedding. Dear Rosie.

☆ ☆ ☆ ☆

The plane to London was delayed by more than two hours. Eventually, passengers were embarked. I found myself standing in the middle of the crush just inside the aircraft entrance. I addressed in a serious tone the hostess who was pinned against the cabin storage rack.

"I was getting married, you know, at eleven o'clock today. I've just telephoned my fiancée and she said she wouldn't wait. That's what you get for not being on time." The hostess smiled at me politely. I put on my glasses. "I told her you were responsible and gave her your name and address."

The hostess was not sure how to respond. She again smiled politely and pointed out my seat. "First class this way, sir."

I have learnt to rely upon madness too often. It will not dissipate easily for me. For Bob, it must not dissipate. It is his sole means of survival. It is injected even into his works. It makes him hard to live with. I'm the one who had nothing but a jar of Brylcreem in his school desk and that was for greasing my hair back behind my ears like flat rats' tails to avoid having to get it cut. I was the waster; the one who could not be taught; the one who boasted he would be a rock 'n' roll star; the one who had to do it for almost everyone else.

"Now I'll have to take an ad out in the paper," I said to the hostess. "WANTED: WARM WOMAN FOR MAN WITHOUT JACKET."

"Hey mister! bring us back a parrot!" the kids used to shout at the men working the barges on the Grand Canal. Am I left forever looking for the parrot?